BAD BOY HOLIDAY

A Bad Boy Inc Story

EVE LANGLAIS

Produced in Canada

Published by Eve Langlais - www.EveLanglais.com

eBook ISBN: 978 177 384 1748

Print ISBN: 978 177 384 175 5

CHAPTER ONE

Winters the Iceman was a grumpy fucking soul, with a well-honed knife, a hidden gun, and an attitude darker than coal.

LYING FLAT ON THE ROOFTOP, MATHIAS WINTERS lined up his sight on his target, Enrico Mazari. Mob boss. All-around asshole. Sitting down in a nice restaurant for dinner with his family. How nice for him. What about all the families he'd destroyed?

Not that Mathias really cared about the nameless and faceless strangers destroyed by this piece of shit.

He got a cool million on accepting the job. He'd get another once he iced the prick. This very public killing was to be a message. A bold warning to others who thought they could get away with worse than murder.

The dining establishment had great big windows and a prominent downtown location, which meant it was busy, especially this time of year. The end-of-year holidays always filled restaurants with people. Hopefully nobody moved when he fired, or that would be unfortunate.

Enrico Mazari stood, wine glass in hand, ready to make a toast. His wife sat to his left. His children beamed at their daddy.

They'd be traumatized for life. This would teach them that a life of crime didn't pay. Unless you were an assassin for hire. Then it was really lucrative.

At times like these, when Mathias made the world a better place, he even felt good about what he was doing. Not enough to melt his frozen heart though. He inhaled.

Exhaled as he pulled the trigger.

The bullet sheared through the glass and hit Enrico between the eyes. The man wavered on his feet, but Mathias didn't wait to see him fall. Not much point. Even a zombie wouldn't rise from that shot.

Job done, he packed up his stuff: gun, tripod, and his concealing hood. Everything went into his shopping bag with a fluffy bear on top before he left the rooftop.

As Mathias skipped down the steps, he removed his dark coat and flipped it inside out to show a light gray. He slipped on a pair of glasses and placed a navy blue tuque on his head. By the time he reached the main floor, he looked like any other harried husband, doing some last-minute shopping.

Just in case, the fake driver's license in his wallet bore the name Larry Arbuckle.

Boy was that perception far from the truth.

He joined the people in the multi-story mall, most of them spilling out onto the sidewalk and road, drawn by the sirens. Emergency vehicles arrived, their flashing lights almost as garish as the lights strung along the street.

Fucking Christmas. A commercially driven joke, which was why he didn't mind taking a job this time of year.

Assassins didn't take holidays.

Ignoring the commotion on the street, Mathias walked two blocks to his rental, which had been paid for in cash and using his fake ID. The gloves he wore wouldn't leave prints. His hair had been lightly sprayed so as to not shed.

A few miles away, he stopped on a dark street and packaged his gun before dropping it into a slot for prepaid package delivery. The cash transaction would leave no trail, and the present would make life a little more annoying to the prick who'd scratched Mathias's car in a parking lot back home.

Mathias abandoned his rental at the airport, boarded his flight, and, by midnight, was asleep in his own bed. He slept soundly and without dreams because only shitty assassins had regrets.

The next morning over coffee and a perfectly cooked egg with a side of ham and avocado, he accepted his next job. By that afternoon, he was on a flight to Colorado. He had a car service drive him from the airport to a snow-covered ski town where the amount of goodwill and cheer made him itch to shoot something.

The carolers that disturbed his dinner were what shoved him over the edge. Later that night, when everyone in the hotel was asleep, he crept outside to relieve some holiday pressure. The stupid inflatable Santa with its jolly smile died, but he left the snowman next door—with his corncob pipe and his button nose—alone.

CHAPTER TWO

Let it snow! Let it snow! Let it snow! – said NO ONE, ever!

THE GUST OF WIND CAUGHT BLAKE AS SHE walked out the main door of the office building, darting up her skirt, giving her a chill despite the thick tights she wore. This time of year she didn't shave. Winter was a time to let that hair grow long enough to braid. It wasn't as if anyone but her cat would see her pasty legs. Which said a lot about her dating life. Lack of it, that was. In her defense, she'd not been living here long.

Her scarf, only loosely placed around her neck, lifted. As she grabbed it, her foot slipped, and then her other boot lost traction. Before she knew it, she was in danger of doing the splits. It might have gotten ugly, and truly painful, if she'd not been saved by a passing stranger.

"Whoa, there, little lady," the man drawled as he

caught her under the arms and hauled her to her feet.

A peek showed a rugged countenance to match. Holy handsome.

Way out of her league, and of course, he'd caught her at her best. "Thanks for saving me."

"You wouldn't want to bust that pretty face."

Pretty? Probably something he said to all the ladies. That didn't stop her from smiling at him. "Too late for that. As you've noted, I'm clumsy." Athletics wasn't her strong suit. Actually, even walking could be a challenge at times when her feet chose to tangle.

"Let's blame gravity." He winked as he steadied her then moved a step back, giving her some space. He was distinguished with his gray peacoat covering a lean body. His dark hair remained in place, combed with neat precision, defying the nipping breeze.

"Also known as my greatest enemy." Tied with her mouth, which kept opening and saying the dumbest things.

"And here I'd have called it a friend, given it allowed me to help a lovely lady in a storm."

"You must be a visitor if you think this is a storm," she joked. Poorly, yet he still chuckled.

"You caught me. I'm more of southern states kind of guy."

She nodded. "You must have come for the

skiing. I hear we have some of the best around." Not that she knew personally. Again, the whole uncoordinated thing.

"I doubt I'll hit the slopes. I am only here for a few days on business." Again, he flashed those pearly whites. Was he flirting with her?

She probably imagined it. "Hope you enjoy the city."

She went to take her leave, but he wasn't ready to let her go. "Will you allow me to walk you to your vehicle?"

"I'm actually taking the bus." She pointed down the street at the plastic shelter with the sign sporting the bus route number.

"A bus in this weather?" He eyed the slippery streets.

A shrug lifted her shoulders. "Don't really have a choice." Her car was in the shop and would be until a part arrived.

"Allow me to arrange a ride for you." He pulled a phone from his pocket, and she arched a brow.

"While I appreciate the gesture, I have to decline." He might be handsome, but as a woman, she knew the unspoken rules to keep herself safe.

"You can pay me back if it's about money."

"Actually, it's more about me giving you my address, which is a no-no with strangers," she sang, almost wagging her finger. "Not to mention, I don't ride alone in cars with people I don't know. It's safer for a lady that way." She winked.

"Are you always this paranoid?" he asked, slipping the phone back into his coat.

"It's called being cautious."

"Must make dating difficult."

"What makes you think I'm single?" The assumption pursed her lips.

He eyed her hand.

"A lack of a ring doesn't mean I'm not in a relationship."

"No ring indicates whatever your status, it's not fully committed." His turn to grin, and it was as bright as the gaudy tree set up in the lobby of her apartment building.

"Does that apply to you too?" she asked, eyeing his hand, seeing no tan line that would indicate he'd recently removed one.

"I'm single. You?"

She should have said, "None of your business." Instead her mouth had other ideas. "I'm not currently dating, nor interested." This close to the holidays would only be awkward. Should she get him a gift? What if she did and he had nothing for her in return?

"How about eating? You do still eat, don't you?" he asked, more persistent than expected.

"That is the oldest and lamest pickup line in the book," she declared.

"Because it is tried and true. By having dinner, we can meet in a public place of your choosing so you're comfortable."

"Sounds good except for one thing."

"What?"

"It involves eating with you. I'm not interested in casual dating, and you've already said you're only here for a few days, meaning you're looking for a fling, and I don't do flings. At all." Although he was handsome enough she almost wanted to forget that personal edict.

"I was just looking for some companionship at dinner. Nothing more."

"Said every pushy guy ever." She rolled her shoulders. "Still not interested, which is why I'm going to say goodbye now."

"I'm sorry to have offended you. Have a good evening." He inclined his head.

"Merry Christmas," she called out as she headed for her stop, hoping in her haste to catch the approaching bus that she didn't fall and land on her face or butt.

She made it onto the mass transit vehicle without mishap. A peek through the window as she found a seat meant she saw him staring at her then saluting her with a half-wave and a smile.

Maybe she should have said yes to dinner. And dragged him home for dessert.

CHAPTER THREE

Winters the Iceman is a murderer they say. He was made to fight and takes great delight in sending you on your way.

SOUNDLY REJECTED. IF MATHIAS WAS THE KIND to give a shit, it might have been ego shattering, but he honestly didn't give a fuck. He'd not come to this skiers' delight of a town for pleasure but business.

After she left, on a bus of all things—disgusting mode of transportation that he only took in the direst circumstance—he glanced at the building she'd emerged from. It was several stories high, with a security guard manning reception inside. Side-by-side elevators plus opposing sets of stairs for entry to the upper levels. Only one staircase remained unlocked at all times for everyone's use. The other one was supposedly under repair. Had been for months, according to the intel he'd gathered.

Rather than go inside, he kept walking. His

hotel wasn't far away, the downtown core full of the things he needed, like a liquor store, restaurant with some excellent Brazilian food, and a hardware store to buy the items he couldn't bring on the plane. Rope. Carabiners. A screwdriver and a rechargeable drill, which he needed for the battery. No need to pay a fortune for fancy toys that might get spotted by TSA security when the basics did the trick.

Supplies acquired, and initial scouting mission accomplished, he headed up to his room, the penthouse of course, giving him the best view. As he stripped, he dropped his clothes onto a chair and paced his room, trying to keep his thoughts on the job. He didn't quite manage it because he found himself strangely distracted by the woman with the wide smile and sassy attitude.

Pity she'd not said yes to dinner. She'd had nice lips, full and inviting. Her figure, hidden under her coat, hinted at curves. A woman with meat on her bones, just the way he liked it. And while he'd sensed her interest in him as a man, she'd not wavered in her decision to brush him off.

Perhaps she'd lied and had a significant other. An idea that didn't sit well at all. Why did it matter? Why the interest in her?

Sure, it had been awhile since he'd had any interest in the opposite sex. Too long, which might be why the memory of this stranger aroused. He was horny. Plain and simple.

Since he had time to kill, he sat in a chair, legs partially spread, head tilted back. Hand on his hardening dick. It thickened in his grip, especially as he recalled the woman's pert replies. If she'd only known she was talking to a killer, her expression would have been much different and probably not as sexy.

But he wasn't the type to get off on fear. He preferred a woman unafraid to smile. Someone who could joke about her almost-mishap with a bright tone and sparkling eyes.

Would she have that same sassy grin during sex? Or would she be the type to moan as he played with her breasts? Which led to him wondering what kind she hid. Large nipples? Small? Pink? Dark? He liked them all. Especially when pushed together that he might slide his cock between them and poke it at a pair of lips.

He could picture her sucking him, taking his tip. He slid his hand up and down his cock at the thought. When he imagined her licking the pearl glistening at the tip, he pumped even faster.

Did she have a full ass, the kind to cushion a man if he took her from behind?

Or he could have her lying down, legs spread and welcoming, breasts peeking, lips parted, expression sultry, watching him as he slid his prick into her pink pussy. Pushing into her as she gasped, moaned. Called his name as she came.

Mathias.

He came, catching the juice with the tissues he'd thought to grab, but it was only as he flushed that he inwardly grumbled about how his fantasy ended.

Why would a woman, a stranger, calling out his real name be so sexy? So desirable?

Could he finally have gotten tired of living in the shadows? Mathias Winters, aka Iceman, who cared about nothing but the balance in his bank accounts.

Nah.

Mathias composed himself and shoved all thoughts of her out of his mind. It wasn't as if he'd ever see her again. Their meeting was happenstance.

Rather than rehash it yet again, he loaded the schematics of this block, and the ones surrounding the hotel, including the one with that office building, into his laptop. He'd already mapped his course. Still, studying it again helped to steady him. He went over his routes. Plan A was the most favorable, but he'd also implemented backups in case things weren't as they seemed.

As the hour for his departure neared, he dressed all in black, form-fitting so that no loose fabric could get caught on anything. Soft-soled, grippy shoes. Gloves. A full-on baklava that only had an opening for his eyes, over which he placed night vision goggles.

He didn't exit the hotel via the hall outside his room. Opening his door would leave a record, and there were cameras on every level. The very lack of activity would provide an alibi if he ever needed it. Not that he planned to get caught.

The balcony outside his room had a high railing, but even better, it proved to be an easy climb to the roof. In this dense area of downtown, the buildings sat close together, which gave him a clear run to the building across from his target. He wasn't about to go through the front doors. Again, too many digital eyes watching. In this era of technology, missions that required proximity proved harder and harder to accomplish.

He chose to enter via a less visible method. The rope he'd bought was tied into a lasso. He swirled and twirled it before flinging it across and watching it drop. It took three tries before it snared the solid metal ventilation chimney. He tugged to tighten it before wrapping and tying it off on his end. Then it was a simple matter of crossing hand over hand to the other side.

While the roof appeared empty, he still crouched upon arriving and scanned the area with his goggles. A camera would emit a slight heat signature because of the wiring. Just like a person would emit a much larger warm spot.

The chance of running into anyone up here would be slim, though. This rooftop wasn't set up for public use even though it had a heated surface for melting snow and ice. It never failed to astonish him how many building owners neglected this point of entry. The door, made of utility metal, had a plain lock that wasn't even engaged.

He checked for any wiring that would indicate an alarm of some kind. Nada.

The target office was only a single flight down; however, he went down two more stories, noting the single camera watching. It rotated slow enough he could easily bypass its digital eye.

Only when he reached the door on the first floor did he have to pause out of sight while he waited for the camera to swing. As it traversed slowly, he waited for his chance.

He needed to distract from his true objective. When the camera went past, he picked the locked door and, when it clicked, shoved it open, triggering an alarm. He shut the door and then moved as quickly as he could up the stairs, hearing the door at the bottom of the stairwell open. The thump of boots indicated someone coming up the stairs. A man, judging by the deep timbre.

"Nothing on the camera, but the security system

shows the door opening and closing," the guard said. "I don't see anyone. Going to check inside." As expected, the guard would do a full sweep of that level.

He waited about thirty seconds, long enough for the guard to have started his search, before triggering the second-floor lock. On his way up to the third floor, he had to hide in the stairwell as the guard emerged more quickly than expected to check on the newest alarm.

The moment the guard went into the floor below his, Mathias bolted back down and set off the first floor again before heading inside. He crossed the office space, barely noticing the display of interior decorating, intent on the Exit sign at the far end, locked and with a sign saying, Closed for Repair.

He set off an alarm going through it and noticed the stairwell didn't have the same security, with wires dangling where a camera should be. He saw no other signs of construction. This staircase went down one extra flight to the basement and the electrical panel for the building.

Mathias pulled out a sealed plastic bag and tossed a few things on the floor. Syringe. Candy wrappers. A few cigarette butts. Making it seem someone had been squatting to do drugs as opposed to anything more nefarious.

Only once he'd set a fake stage did he turn off the power. Lights off didn't mean he was in the dark. His goggles filtered the shadows enough for him to navigate. He quickly went up the stairs to the top floor, an ear peeled in case the guard didn't do as expected.

The fact there was a guard at all surprised him. Why did a building of real estate and other home-related shit have a need for paid security?

Why, indeed, he wondered as he noticed the lock on the third floor possessed an electronic keypad, unlike the others. It also still had juice. It obviously relied on a backup supply in case of a power failure.

A good thing he'd brought more tools. The battery he'd brought, an 18-volt rechargeable for a drill, gave him some juice once he attached wires to it, then the lock. It shorted, probably setting off yet another alarm. But the guard wouldn't pay attention to it given he had bigger problems. Right now, he was having to maneuver in the dark.

Mathias entered the target area and was glad to see the power source didn't extend to anything else inside. The camera above the door was dead, but it wouldn't stay that way. He needed to move fast.

The office appeared much like any other successful business with short carpet on the floors and many closed doors with gleaming plaques inscribed with names.

He knew them all. After all, he'd done his research. Looked up the employees best he could and found them on social media, in government records. Everything appeared on the up and up. No criminal records. Nothing untoward to be seen, which to him rang false.

Everyone working here seemed too perfect. Which probably explained why he'd been hired to go after the owner himself. The elusive Hugo Laurentian, who'd recently set up BBI Realty offices around the world. A man rarely seen in person.

Originally, Mathias had planned to visit the guy in the Caribbean, which he called home, but he'd gotten a tip that Laurentian would be in town for Christmas with his wife, closing a deal on a chalet.

Which chalet? And when would Laurentian be showing up to finalize the sale? Once Mathias got that information, he'd plan his next move.

Despite his many violent skills, he wasn't expected to kill anyone. On the contrary, the person who hired him simply wanted a package delivered. A small box with only a broken watch inside. He knew because he'd looked. Run it through a scanner to make sure he wasn't carrying around some kind of radioactive bomb. Nothing about the watch or box set off any alarms. Meaning the gift was about the object itself. Given Hugo had lots of money, he was going to assume blackmail.

Not his problem. His instructions were to deliver the box into Hugo's hand. Easy money.

None of the computers would load, the power

still not having come back on. Even if they had, he didn't have the time to hack one, plus add the fact no reputable company actually had any hard drives on site. They all relied on servers and clouds to save information. It should be noted he was more old school when it came to information gathering. He disliked the internet but used it if necessary. Problem being most of the world had moved away from hard copies. And their firewalls were getting better and better.

He couldn't find a single filing cabinet. Paper appeared scarce in this modern office. It wasn't until he reached the reception area that he finally got a clue.

A spiral-bound calendar sat on the surface with notes penciled in. Tuesday, pick up dry cleaning for Blake. Thursday, get Mom's present. And then he saw it.

Office Christmas party. What were the chances the owner of the company, who was planning to be in town, wouldn't appear?

The lights suddenly came on, and he quickly shut his eyes and shoved at his goggles. He remained crouched behind the reception desk. The security system, including the cameras, would have to be brought back online. He probably had a minute or two before that happened. He stood and began moving for the stairs he'd used to enter, only to freeze as he heard the distinctive beep as the alarm system came online and then, more astonishing, the sweeping red lights. Motion sensor beams, the kind he couldn't hope to avoid.

What the fuck? Did this company think their land deals were state secrets? And more importantly, how to get out without getting caught?

He eyed the strobing lights and remembered the placement of the cameras on his way in. No way to hide his exit, which meant the company would be alerted as to an intruder, and he might have just screwed his mission. If the mysterious Mr. Laurentian heard, he might cancel his plans, and there went his easy money.

There had to be a way out of here. He could only think of one. It involved subtly putting out a foot and triggering a motion sensor out of camera view. The guard would either have to turn off the alarm to investigate or chalk it up to more wonkiness and reset.

No alarm sounded. Had it not sensed his foot? He poked it again, more thoroughly this time, through the red beam.

Then he waited.

It took that lazy fucker fifteen minutes to come looking. Mathias readied himself as he heard the lock to the main office door being disengaged. The person entered and jangled some keys. A second later, he heard the *beep, beep, beep* as they keyed in a sequence that removed the motion sensing beams.

"Stupid glitching alarm system," muttered a female voice. A familiar one.

Could it be?

He peeked around the counter's edge, and there she was, dressed in yoga pants that clung to rounded thighs and a bubble butt, tossing a jacket on a chair. Her ribbed sweater, with its snowflake pattern, bunched just above the swell of her hips, filled out nicely by her chest.

Shit, he was staring.

He practically threw himself behind the barrier, his heart racing.

His heart didn't race.

He had nerves of steel. Ice in his veins.

A hard-on in his pants.

Fuck.

What was she doing here?

She works here, dumbass.

Obviously, but how did she get here so quickly? Surely there weren't many buses running at two a.m.

Lights flipped on, making it even harder to hide. It wasn't easy to keep track of her, and yet he had a sixth sense of her location. Instinct had him crab-walking around the counter as she went behind it. A game of cat and mouse.

Her phone rang. "Hello." A pause. "I took a taxi and am at the office right now about to check." She tapped a few keys, muttering, "Hold your horses and give me a second to see if the cameras caught anything." Another pause of silence. "No, Norris didn't come up with me. He's still checking the first and second floors. Apparently, they were the ones that glitched out first. If you ask me, it's that damned mouse I've been telling you about." She was quiet for a second before chuckling. "Well, either it's a mouse and we need an exterminator, or one of you jerks ate my last candy bar.

"Yeah, yeah, sure you didn't take it. Whatever," she teased, her amused lilt making him wonder who she spoke to in such a friendly manner. "I'm going to hang up now because I need coffee and a donut. Make that two donuts." The chair creaked as she rose, muttering, "Yes, I will call you if I see anything. Bye." The phone hit the desk, and she walked away toward the break room he'd seen during his quick search.

This was his chance to escape.

Only as he stood, he saw her phone on the counter, screen unlocked since it hadn't been inactive long enough.

He couldn't resist opening her contact list. Lifting his wrist, he only had to flex it to take pictures as he scrolled.

He heard her singing and banging around. How long would it take to make her coffee?

Not long enough. He closed the contact app and then sprinted for the nearest stairwell. He held the door to slow its closing and minimize the click as it latched. He paused to see if she'd notice. Heard nothing so he exited the same way he entered, heading for the rooftop and his rope. He untied it from the chimney and ran for the edge with it clipped to the harness he wore over his black outfit. As he swung over the gap to the next building, he waited to see if anyone noticed his presence and shouted.

He hit the other building with his soft-soled shoes and then climbed up. Within ten minutes, he was back in his hotel room, masturbating as he imagined her eating the donut off his dick.

CHAPTER FOUR

It's the most wonderful time of the year; unless you're single and buying presents for yourself.

He's stalking me, was the first thing Blake thought when he walked in to the office lobby the next day. Of course it would be while she was fixing the Christmas garland hanging off the front counter, hand waving madly because of the tape that was stuck to it.

His appearance caused a bit of a flutter. The handsome stranger had come looking for her. Flattering, or a sign he was a psycho? Even if the latter, it was still kind of sexy.

But this was her place of work.

Wrenching the ruined tape from her skin, she dropped it into the garbage pail, missed, then stepped on it, making a crinkling noise as she rounded the reception desk to intercept him. She ordered her flip-flopping tummy to ignore his slowly emerging smile. She also resisted the urge to bend over and wrestle some more with the tape that hated her. "What are you doing here?"

"I would ask the same of you. What a surprise."

She focused on the lie to ignore the seductive quality of that granite countenance. "Please. We both know this isn't a coincidence. I thought I made myself clear. I'm not interested." She grabbed Mr. Handsome by the arm and steered him in the direction of the elevator.

"I know you did, and yet, fate appears to have other plans."

She snorted. "You are not a guy to believe in fate."

"On the contrary, I do. Me running into you has to be karma." He flashed a smile and a smoldering gaze that warmed her down to the toes.

"No, it's called being pushy. You can't be here."

"And yet I am and getting the distinct impression you're trying to get rid of me."

"What gave it away?" was her mocking rejoinder.

"It seems you're suffering from a misunderstanding."

"What's to misunderstand? You don't know how to accept no as an answer, which some women might find cute, but it gives me an urge to report you to authorities for harassment."

His brows rose. "Harassment? I've done nothing."

"You call being here nothing?"

"I'm here because I have an appointment."

She gaped at him. "Wait a second, are you Larry Arbuckle?" Because he sure didn't look the way she expected. A guy like him should have a name like Malcolm Steele or one like those famous models.

"I am Mr. Arbuckle. Here to meet with Blake Jenners."

She felt all kinds of stupid for her accusation. "Ah shoot. I'm sorry. I'm so embarrassed now." Indeed, her cheeks heated, a surely lovely shade of tomato red. Some women looked coy and cute when they blushed. She appeared to be having an allergic reaction.

To his credit he ignored the fact her face might explode. He smiled, looking perfectly put together, with every hair in place—a temptation that demanded ruffling—jaw smooth shaven, pea coat not holding a single speck of lint. "Perhaps as an apology, you'll now have dinner with me."

The guy never stopped trying. "Still not interested." She turned before he could see the lie. "Nor is it allowed because of company rules." She led the way down a carpeted hall to a door missing a plaque.

She didn't knock before opening and knew what he'd see the moment he walked in: a modest-sized space with a wooden desk, a sideboard with a display of flowers, and a pair of chairs. Not the deep plush ones seen in the bigger offices. Not for the newest associate.

Arbuckle glanced up the hall before following her inside. He inclined his head toward the empty chair behind the desk. "Is Mr. Jenners running late?"

Just as she was about to correct Mr. Arbuckle, he turned and wandered to the wall to look at the degrees.

She waited. Noticed his frown.

"Hey, how is it that, according to the BBI Realty website, Mr. Jenners is listed as having been in the real estate game since being licensed in nineteen eighty-three. And yet this"—he jabbed a finger at the framed document on the wall—"is dated less than five years ago." He spun as he finished asking.

She took a seat behind the desk. "Because that's my degree."

"You're Blake Jenners?"

"If I were a son, you'd add junior," she remarked, hands folded in front of her.

"I didn't realize... None of the company info indicated he had a daughter." His brow remained creased.

"An error on our part. I've only recently begun working here for my dad. They haven't updated the website yet."

"I see."

"Is working with me going to be a problem?"

She kept her tone level and measured, as he continued to have a serious mien.

"Yes," he admitted finally.

Before she could tell him to shove his misogyny, he said the one thing to steal her voice. "If we work together, then we can't have dinner."

"On the contrary. We can have dinner. Lunch. Even breakfast if you like," she sang with a smile. "We just won't be doing anything other than eating and business." No sleeping with clients. Ever.

"Is that a dare?" he asked in a deep rumble.

"Most certainly not."

"Maybe I should mention the fact I don't always like to follow the rules."

"You will if you intend to do business with us."

"You mean do business with you."

"Are you incapable of seeing women as anything other than sex objects?"

He coughed before managing a raspy, "I assure you it's never been a problem before."

"Meaning what?" She suffered under no illusions. She was pretty, yes, but not a thin girl by any means. Not fat either, just padded all over. Big boned as they used to say.

"Meaning there is something about you, Blake, that I find very intriguing."

She startled, mostly because he sounded surprised. As if he couldn't figure it out either. "I'm sure you won't think that once you get to know me."

"On the contrary, the more you talk, the more I find myself fascinated. And attracted." His gaze wandered, and she squirmed in her seat.

The man truly was too sexy for his own good.

He was also trying too hard. It made no sense. She cleared her throat. "Mr. Arbuckle."

"Larry."

"Mr. Arbuckle," she enunciated. "I take it by your continued insistence on flirting that we won't be able to work together." She stood. "I'll see if I can find someone else to handle you."

"Don't bother. I want you."

She knew he meant for real estate, and yet there was that stupid flutter again. "If you wish to hire me as your agent, then you'll have to stop flirting."

"Why?" Again, he smiled, and the tingle spread.

"Because it's not appropriate."

"Not appropriate would be me kissing you."

Her lips rounded. Why did he have to suggest it? Her gaze went to his mouth. She mentally shook herself. "No kissing."

"Unless there's mistletoe, then it's kind of mandatory."

She rolled her eyes. "Fine." She wondered where to find some mistletoe. She cleared her throat. "Now that we've come to an agreement, let's talk properties."

"No need. I already emailed about the one I'm interested in."

"The Grizzly Lake Chalet has been sold."

"Conditionally," he remarked.

She frowned. "How do you know that? It's not general knowledge."

"I have my ways. The fact there are conditions still pending means I have wiggle room."

"Barely. I expect to hear it's been sold in the next few days. There are other properties I can show you."

He shook his head. "I know what's on the market. I don't want them. I want the Grizzly."

"You know what Mick Jagger says."

"I do. And I'm still going to insist on seeing the place."

Since he couldn't actually buy it, it wouldn't hurt to show him. After all, the owner wasn't in residence. Hadn't been for years. They'd had to stage the home for showings.

"Tell you what, I'll show you the chalet, but keep in mind you won't be able to buy unless the other deal falls through." Which didn't seem likely. Then again, who asked for a home inspection on a home worth five point seven million? The buyer even wanted a survey done on the possibility of avalanches.

"When can we go?"

"How about right now?"

"And how will we get there? Because I don't ride the bus." There was a taunt in the query.

She had the reply. "We'll take my car, of course."

"Since when do you drive?"

"Since the garage finally got the missing part and fixed it. I picked it up last night."

"What happened to not driving with strange men?"

"That was yesterday when you were the creepy guy I met on the sidewalk. Today, I know your name and where you live. So does Becky at the front desk."

"In other words, no killing you and dumping the body?"

If he'd meant to shock her, he'd failed. "Given I know the city better, chances are it's you they'd never find."

The threat only made him laugh louder.

She checked in with Becky on the way out, and while the receptionist did her best to flirt, he appeared immune. Which surprised her. Becky had the kind of looks men drooled over.

Yet, he only had eyes for Blake.

Kind of surreal.

He followed her to the paid lot across the street, only to hesitate beside her baby blue Mini Countryman. He perused it with a skeptical eye. "Are you sure we'll both fit?"

"It's more spacious than it looks."

"I thought large vehicles were a prerequisite for a realty job?"

"Not if you want to save the planet," she quipped, sliding in behind the steering wheel.

"If I'd have known we'd be riding in a clown car, I would have rented something to drive for the day."

"You think I'd let you chauffeur me?" she queried.

"I'm excellent behind the wheel."

For a moment she eyed him then smiled as she said, "I bet you go too fast." It was meant as a double entendre to prick his ego.

His lips quirked. "Only for the first few seconds, then I slow down and enjoy the ride."

She squeezed her thighs together. She wouldn't think about him riding between them. Keep it on a business level. Her wet panties ignored that advice.

"What's your interest in the Grizzly Lake property?" she asked as she pulled out onto the main road.

"Is this the question period where you find out my must-haves, my dislikes, and suggest other places?"

"It's good to have options."

"None of those options will have a backyard going down to one of the nicest lakes in the region with fishing almost year-round."

"There is public access for those who don't live right on it."

"I prefer to have privacy when I'm relaxing. There's also the view. That house sits high and overlooks that lake with no nearby neighbors."

"If that's your criteria, then I've got a lovely mountain-view home for half the price and with more square footage."

"Does it have a river stone fireplace extending two stories?"

"I know a mason who can build one."

"Massive entertaining deck with hot tub?"

"Tiny details," she scoffed.

"The master bedroom has a floor-to-ceiling window that makes it seem like you're floating in the sky."

"Needs frequent cleaning because of the birds hitting it."

"You really don't want me to like this place. Why?" he asked.

"Because I think you're wasting your time. The place is practically sold."

"I still want to see it."

"Why bother since you already know everything about it?"

"Think of it as getting an idea of what I like if I do agree to see other places."

"We could have done that in my office with a slideshow."

"Where's the adventure in that?"

The drive was more than forty minutes, as they had to leave the city and drive into the mountains. At least the weather remained clear and the roads free of ice. Snow laced the trees and frosted the peaks. When they finally crested the last hill, she had to admit he had a point about the view.

The house was built on a bluff overlooking the lake with a lift that could bring people up and down since stairs were unfeasible. The house itself had the stone and cedar exterior many chalets adopted but on a massive scale. Big wood beams, a peaked roof that helped with heavy snow, more than a few chimneys because it wasn't just the great room that had a fireplace.

She exited the car and waited for him, breathing in the fresh air, feeling the crisp cold on her cheeks.

"Beautiful," he breathed, only he was looking at her.

"Shall we go inside?" she asked while texting Becky to let her know she'd reached the chalet.

Arbuckle stood to the side as she punched the combination into the lock. They entered a vast entry hall, the stone tile covered in a rug to catch snow and dirt.

"Shoes and boots off," she said, leaning over to unzip hers.

When she stood, wearing only her stockings, it

was to see him staring at her. She arched a brow. "Something wrong?"

"No," was his gruff reply. He kicked off his shoes.

"Where would you like to begin?"

"How about right here?" He poked his head inside a door. "I take it this is the home office." With that statement, he began walking through the various rooms.

She said nothing as he checked it out and, instead, watched him. Tried to read his expression as he toured the office then the kitchen. Barely paused in the dining room.

She thought her awareness of him in the car was because of the proximity. Not even a foot between them. Yet, despite the massive space around them, she remained on edge. Tingling. Anticipating... nothing. For all his flirting words, he never did anything untoward.

It was almost maddening. Had all that talk just been about seeing this house? Trying to butter her up to see if he could steal it from their other client? As if that would happen.

He spent only a moment in the sunken living room with the massive fireplace and windows overlooking the deck before heading to the second floor with the master bedroom.

The bed faced those windows, but he didn't spare it a glance as he went straight for the view. "It really is magnificent. But I can't buy it," he said, shoving his hands into his pockets.

"No kidding."

"Not because of the conditional offer. I can't buy it or any other houses from you." He turned to face her, looking entirely too intense.

"Why not?"

"Because if I do, I can't have what I want."

"I don't understand."

"Don't you?" he murmured, moving closer. "I'd rather kiss you."

CHAPTER FIVE

He must have gotten lightheaded up on the mountain bluffs, because he only meant to charm her when her panties came right off.

GIVEN ALL HER REBUFFS, HE'D NOT EXPECTED HIS comment to work. He'd begun to wonder if he'd mistaken her red cheeks for something else.

He didn't usually have to work this hard to charm. Yet, she seemed impervious.

So he'd boldly stated what he wanted, and for once, he wasn't faking it. Unfortunately, the desire was all too real from the moment he'd seen her wearing a bright red sweater dress with candy canes patterned all over, snug around her curves, belted at the waist. Her calf-high leather boots sexy as all fuck. Even sexier? When she unzipped and removed them, showing her stocking-covered feet.

He wanted nothing more than to crawl up that dress and—

She kissed him!

He was so startled it took him a moment before

he had the sense to kiss her back. A hot, passionate kiss that saw them suddenly pulling apart and staring at each other. Her with cheeks flushed. Hell, he wasn't far off himself.

"I shouldn't have done that," she remarked.

"I disagree."

"You're leaving in a few days."

"I am." No point in lying.

She licked her lips. He was jealous of her tongue. She saw him staring. "It would just be sex."

Would it just be sex? It had to be. She was a complication he didn't need in his perfect life. "Have dinner with me."

"I don't need dinner to kiss you." She pointed to the flowers on her dress. "Mistletoe."

He took a moment to process what she'd said then grinned. "We mustn't break tradition." He swept her into his arms, lifting her, holding her close.

She cupped his face, nibbling and sucking at his mouth, her breath hot and minty. The feel of her curves was soft and pleasing. She parted her lips and invited his tongue. Twined it with his. Sucked at him, and he felt it down to his fucking toes.

But mostly in his cock. He throbbed something fierce.

The woman could kiss, but he wanted more than that.

The bed was close, the window even closer. He

pressed her against it, hands grabbing at her full ass, kneading it. He ground himself against her, wanting nothing more than to strip and slide into her.

Too fast.

Even for him.

It didn't stop him from trailing hot kisses along the edge of her jaw to the lobe of her ear. He bit the lobe lightly, and a shudder went through her. A gentle bite had her moaning.

He sucked it for a second longer before moving his lips down the smooth skin of her neck. The scent of her tickled him, the taste of her flesh delighted. Her dress impeded his access, but he appreciated the oversized buttons holding it closed. He only had to undo a couple to reveal her breasts restrained in a sturdy bra. The kind that probably had a dozen hooks in the back. Easier to just shove the cup aside and bare her to his touch.

She gasped as he nipped first one nipple then the other. They protruded. Demanded more attention. He was more than happy to give it. He leaned forward and caught the hard buds in his mouth one by one, sucking them, teasing them, even biting down, making her cry out.

For all she shivered and moaned, he wasn't in as much control as he'd like. He wanted badly to thrust and come between those perfect thighs.

The lack of control froze him. This had already gone too far.

And it was about to go further because she whispered, "Touch me."

There wasn't a man alive who could have said no to that soft request.

With a groan of surrender, he claimed her lips for a torrid kiss. While one hand kept her anchored in place against the window, the other went exploring, gliding up her stockinged leg to realize the stockings didn't end in garters. She wore the full bottom kind, practical, but still sexy, the fabric damp in the crotch once he managed to wedge his fingers between. He was no better than a clumsy boy as he pulled and finally moved those stockings down and out of his way, the cotton panties loose enough to be shoved aside.

When he touched her hot flesh, she cried out. Hell, he almost cried out as his hips involuntarily thrust.

He couldn't help but plunge two fingers into her, feeling the heat of her sex. The pulse. The squeeze.

She rocked in his grip, grunting, begging, "Yes. Yes. Yes."

He wanted to stop and give her his cock. But he couldn't bring himself to slow the rhythm. Couldn't stop himself from watching her, with her eyes shut, her lips parted, flushed and wanton in that moment.

About to come for him.

When she orgasmed, it squeezed his fingers so tight he gasped. Even came a little. Caught her long sigh of pleasure with a kiss.

Was ready to dig out a condom and get working on his own climax when a phone rang, chiming to the tune of "Jingle Bells."

Not his phone. "Ignore it."

"I can't. That's my daddy calling."

CHAPTER SIX

Angels We Have Heard on High; might have sounded like her when she came.

A PART OF HER RESENTED THE INTRUSION OF HER happy, ringing phone. Another part froze in disbelief. What had just happened?

Blake had just thrown caution to the wind and almost had sex with a stranger.

Actually, given she'd come it might still count.

Total error in judgment no matter how good it felt. Still, when he'd said he wanted to kiss her... how could she resist? If he'd been a shitty kisser, she might have been able to stop. But he was a great kisser. And when he touched her...she came apart in his arms.

Came on his hand.

Standing with her bare ass in the window for anyone to see. A glance over her shoulder showed only snowy treetops. Still. Not exactly discreet.

She moved away from him and snared her

phone from her purse on the way, her dress coming down to cover her as she wrestled one-handed to tug her tights and undies back into place. During the heat of the moment, she'd forgotten about her unshaven legs. Luckily, he'd only felt and not seen her very natural bush.

Still putting her outfit to rights, she answered, perhaps a tad more breathless than necessary. "Hello, Daddy."

"Is everything okay, Lakey?" His nickname for her.

"Fine. Just fine. Lots of stairs in the house I'm showing. These legs weren't meant for climbing." She let out a short laugh that sounded very unconvincing.

She glanced at her client—Lover? What should she call him? He stood there looking smug. Odd given she'd been the one to get off, not him.

"Are you still with Mr. Arbuckle?"

"I am. Showing him the Grizzly Lake Chalet."

"Why would you bother? It's sold."

"I know, but he wanted me to see the things he liked about it to get ideas."

"You should have taken him to an available house. Like the Periwinkle Cabin. Or maybe Doe's Retreat?"

"On my list if I can get in to see them later today," she stated, trying to maintain her composure, which wasn't easy given her stockings wanted to slide down and her underwear was wet. Her nipples throbbed, and Daddy kept talking, so she said, “I’m still here with Arbuckle, and I highly doubt he wants to listen to us chat. I’ll see you at the office.”

Before he could refuse, she hung up.

Arbuckle leaned against the window.

“That was my father.”

“You don’t say. I take it he’s not happy you brought me here.”

She rolled a shoulder. “He’d prefer I showed you an available home.”

“I’m ready to go right now if you are.” There was a definite double entendre in his words, but she’d had a moment to find her sanity now that he’d given her some relief.

“Unfortunately, we can’t right now. I’m required at the office.”

“Of course, you are,” he rumbled, striding past her. “And let me guess, tomorrow you’re busy too.”

She couldn’t have said what compelled her to say, “Have dinner with me tonight.”

He stopped by the front door and spun. “Going to try and sell me on another house?”

“No business.” Amended to, “Not entirely business.” She blushed. But she remained resolute. If she was going to have a fling, might as well do it with a guy who made her see stars and would be gone in a few days.

"When and where?"

"There's an Italian place two blocks from my office. Say, seven p.m.?"

"Will that give you enough time to go home and freshen up?"

She pursed her lips. Was that a subtle jibe about her legs needing a shave? Had he noticed it during their tryst? "Saying I don't look good enough?"

"If you wear that dress for dinner, all I'm going to be able to think about is how good it looked around your waist when I was fingering you."

Her knees almost buckled. Crude and sexy at the same time. His wicked smile said he knew exactly how he affected her.

Which might have been why she was saucy enough to say, "It felt even better than you can imagine."

Then she sauntered past him, cheeks hot as he chuckled. "I can't wait for dinner."

Neither could she, which meant the car ride back was torture. Especially since he placed a hand on her leg. Nothing more, yet its weight only served to remind her what he'd done. How it felt.

What would he say if she pulled the car to the side of the road and mauled him?

At his direction, she dropped him off at his hotel, blushed, and said no thanks at his offer to come upstairs. She couldn't, not knowing the hairy state of her body. She called the office and told them she'd ripped her tights when she slipped in the snow. Not the first time it had happened, so no one would question why she went home.

She took a long shower and used a lot of soap. Made a note to get some drain cleaner, too, given the pelt she mowed off.

When she emerged, bare-legged, clean underarms, and very trimmed pubes, it was to see her cat staring at her.

Judging her.

"Don't start, Fluff." Yes, she was that crazy lady who talked to her cat. "You didn't see this guy. He's like sex on a stick."

She just wanted to lick and bite, which had never happened before. Just like she'd never slept with a guy so quickly. Hell, if she was going to be honest, she'd never had a fling.

And here she was, getting ready for sex with an almost veritable stranger.

Assuming dinner would lead to sex. Perhaps he'd cancel. Or he'd claim he was tired. Maybe find someone better. Skinnier. Prettier.

She shook her head at the negative thought. Since when did she care? He hadn't seemed to mind her shape earlier. And it wasn't as if this was anything more than two people hooking up for some fun.

Which meant no regrets.

Given her legs were sensitive, she vetoed the

stockings and put on some pants paired with a pink cashmere sweater threaded with silver snowflakes. She also shoved extra undies into her purse. A good thing because she spent the rest of that day thinking about him. How he'd made her feel. What would happen tonight?

She'd already broken so many rules. And honestly didn't care. She'd never felt so on fire for a man before. Needy. Wanton. Sexy.

He had to be using her. No way was he overcome with lust. Believing that would make it easier to keep her heart out of it. This was just sex. Pleasure.

In a few days he'd be gone. No one hurt.

But she'd be doing a lot of laundry because there went another pair of panties. Seven o'clock took forever to arrive and then came too soon.

Ready. Not ready. She'd never been so nervous before. It didn't help that she'd convinced herself on the walk over that he wouldn't show up.

While she'd chosen the restaurant because of its delicious food, it never occurred to her that the bistro might be romantic with its tablecloths and rounded booths, the lighting dim.

And he was already there. Arbuckle stood as she slid into the booth. He then sat across from her, doing nothing but being elegant and charming. She was the one with her mind in the gutter, constantly staring at his hand. The one that pleasured her.

He growled. "Stop it."

"What?" She cast him a startled glance.

"You make me forget we're in a crowded place. All I want to do is get under that table and enjoy some dessert."

She squirmed. "I don't think that's allowed in public."

"I know," he grumbled. "Doesn't mean I like it."

"About this afternoon..."

"If you say you regret it, I will stab myself with this butter knife." He held it poised.

Her lips curved. "I was going to say I don't usually do that."

"I should hope you don't fool around with all your clients."

"Never. But that's not the only first." The wine loosened her tongue, and she almost slapped a hand on her mouth.

"What else was a first for you, Blake?" He purred her name.

She blushed and ducked her head. "Nothing."

"You've never been fingered?"

She shuddered. "I have." She didn't add not as well as he'd managed. "I meant doing that in someone's house. Standing up," she stammered.

He chuckled. "Don't tell me you're usually in the bed in the dark."

"Isn't that standard?"

"If you can wait that long." He slid over on the

seat. His hand landed on her thigh. "Personally, if we make it out of this restaurant without you coming, I'll be surprised."

Her lips parted. "Mr. Arbuckle."

"Call me Matt."

"Isn't your name Larry?"

"I prefer my middle name with my friends."

"I didn't know we were friends." Her breathing hitched as his hand traveled to the pulsing spot between her thighs.

"Oh, I'd say we are good friends." He pressed, and she shuddered.

But she couldn't let him control the situation this time. She placed her hand on his thigh. Squeezed it. His gaze locked onto hers.

"I have your salad," the waiter interrupted.

She thought it was over, but Matt's right hand stayed where it was. He ate with his left.

Her left hand stayed on his thigh and crept over. She ate with her right. She couldn't hold his stare, so she concentrated on her food. The salad disappeared.

The main course took two hands, and she only ate a little before pushing it away. Her hand was back on his lap, hidden by the table and its cloth. His hand was buried between her thighs.

The cake with whipped cream and fresh berries arrived. Not that she tasted anything when he slid down her zipper, slipped his hand into her pants, and fingered her directly.

Her eyes lost focus as he kept rubbing. The forkful of dessert dangled in front of her mouth, and it took him whispering, "Eat or people will see you coming," for her to climax.

She might have cried out if he'd not taken that moment to kiss her, swallowing any noise she might have made as her orgasm trembled through her, pulsing around the finger he'd inserted.

The cock she held through his slacks throbbed in her grip.

She wanted nothing more than to be somewhere she could have him inside her. She opened her mouth and whispered, "Let's go back to my place."

As he said, "My hotel is closer."

That was when her phone with its usual great timing went off.

CHAPTER SEVEN

Winters the Iceman was confused and so horny. He could flirt all day, even laugh and play, but admitting feelings was corny.

"WHOEVER THAT IS HAS SHIT TIMING," MATHIAS grumbled, more blue-balled than ever. Only the Iceman didn't feel cold. He ran a fever.

"It's actually the alarm for the office. Sorry, I'm going to have to cut our date short."

"You're going to check it out?"

"I'm closest."

It wasn't just arousal that had him saying, "You aren't going alone."

"I'll be fine. It's probably the cleaning staff. And I won't be alone. Security is there."

"I'm coming with you." Perhaps he'd get a chance to find out more about the Christmas party, which, thus far, he'd not broached. Too busy seducing the lovely Blake Jenners. He wanted to lie and say he did it just to milk her for information. The truth was he wanted her something fierce.

"I didn't take you for the hero type."

"More like gentleman."

"I wouldn't have used that word either," she said with a teasing tilt of her lips as she squeezed his leg.

Fuck. Did she realize just how badly his balls ached? "Careful, or we'll be stopping in an alley along the way."

"We can't!" she huffed, spots of color in her cheek.

"Do you really want to dare me?"

Rather than reply, she leaned out and signaled their waiter.

Which led to a power struggle over the check.

"I'm getting it," he declared, reaching for the bill.

She snagged it. "As my client, I insist. It's a business expense."

"This isn't business," he growled. Which wasn't entirely a lie. It might have started out as work, but he'd gone past that the first time he fingered her.

Since she was reaching for her credit card, he threw cash at the waiter. Probably more than needed, but the guy in the suit didn't argue when Mathias said, "Keep the change."

"Matt!" She squeaked his name.

He'd rather she screamed it. "Let's go see what the fuss is about."

He helped her into her coat, showing a courtesy he didn't usually bother with unless playing a role.

Like the one he'd been playing with Blake. Although, was it really a sham? It felt entirely natural to lace his fingers with hers and keep a grip on her hand as they walked the two blocks to her office building. He told himself it was because she kept slipping. Almost tripping.

She chattered on the way, mostly about how it was probably nothing and he could stay downstairs while she reset the alarm.

The moment he saw the empty desk in the vestibule and the coffee cup on the floor, he tucked her behind him. "Something's wrong."

"Ya think?" she muttered. Then more loudly, "Kayla. Are you here?"

He slapped a hand over her mouth. "Shh."

She bit him.

He let go, not because it hurt. Either she got the point to be quiet or she didn't. At least they were still close to the door. Easy to escape if needed. He left the gun inside his coat for now.

Rather than retreat, Blake moved to the reception desk, and he had to follow quickly as she leaned over it, aiming her light. "I found Kayla."

Before he could stop her, she'd scooted around the counter and knelt. He reached her as she placed fingers on the woman's neck. Her uniform was intact. He saw no signs of assault. No blood pooling.

"She's breathing," Blake announced.

"Is she napping?"

"On the job and that deeply?" Blake snorted. "I think she's been knocked out."

"Doubtful someone snuck up on her. I'm going to say sleeping drug, probably dumped in her coffee." He pointed to the cardboard cup with a café logo. It had landed upright, unspilled.

"Why would anyone put Kayla to sleep?"

"To rob the place."

"We don't keep any money in the office."

"Your company doesn't, but what about the others in the building?" Home decoration on the second level. Renovation on the next. With the last floor being BBI Realty.

Blake's lips pursed. "I guess it's possible. Which makes this a crime scene. You should go. I need to call this in." She stood and began to shove him in the direction of the door.

He dug in his heels. "I am not leaving you here alone."

"I'll be fine. I'm calling nine-one-one and requesting an ambulance and the police."

"They'll want my statement."

"To tell them what? That you saw nothing? Go." She kept shoving as she dialed one-handed and put the phone to her ear. She offered him a weak smile as someone answered, and she quickly said, "We need police and paramedics at Nine Elm Street. I think there's been a break-in."

He didn't hear the reply as the door shut behind him. He didn't like leaving her alone inside, but the cops would be coming, and he knew all the exits and entrances to the building. He headed for the alley. No cars parked on the street. Probably meant if someone was still inside, they might have parked nearby.

Or climbed in like he had the night before. That didn't seem likely though given they'd taken the time to knock out the night guard.

It wasn't a car he found but a pair of motorcycles parked in the alley. Crotch rockets made for speed. One could belong to the security guard. But what about the other? Could it be someone else in the vicinity parked it?

Sirens in the distance lifted his head.

He really shouldn't be caught in an alley. He'd been very careful to keep clean. He had no prints or DNA on file. Still, in his line of work, it was best to never be observed in the first place.

Mathias Winters—whose clients and enemies knew as the Iceman—was a wanted man.

As he eased out of the alley, he heard glass shattering. A body hurtled out of the window on the second floor, hitting the dumpster and rolling to the ground. Blake appeared in the open window and paused as if contemplating the jump.

"Don't you dare!" he yelled as he ran back into the alley.

The jumper chose a bike and kicked at the stand. *Vroom.* Off they went like a rocket. If the keys weren't conveniently in the ignition of the second bike for a quick getaway, he probably wouldn't have followed.

But fate intervened, and he couldn't help himself. A purring machine between his legs. Wind streaming. The power and speed to fly.

He weaved in and out of traffic following the other bike, wondering what he was doing. This had nothing to do with his job.

Nothing even to do with Blake. Just him being...

Not a hero. Never a hero.

Nor was he a gentleman.

And apparently, he wasn't even a killer that night because rather than keep following the bike, when it became clear he wouldn't catch it, he headed back for the woman whose scent lingered on his fingers.

Maybe it wasn't too late for dessert.

CHAPTER EIGHT

Forget a silent night, or my orgasmic plight. Nothing is calm or feeling quite bright.

BLAKE WATCHED HIM DRIVE OFF AND REALLY HAD to wonder about Mr. Larry "Matt" Arbuckle.

On paper, he was a serious guy who dealt in hand sanitizer of all things. But he had hidden depths. He had a quiet strength about him. A naughty edge.

And he could ride a motorcycle like he was melded to the machine.

Not what she expected from a guy with leather loafers not suitable for the weather and a peacoat.

Then again, she wasn't how she portrayed herself. She eyed the fellow on the floor. Knocked out cold. The lump on his temple would be a throbbing mass when he woke.

She'd silenced the alarm and now waited in the lobby for the help to arrive. Joleen, another BBI employee, stalked in, wearing head-to-toe leather, high heels, and attitude that went well with her spiked blonde hair.

Joleen arched a brow. "*You* caught a thief?

"I'm just as surprised as you." The moment Matt left Blake in the lobby, she'd heard the stairwell door click shut. Without thinking, she went after the intruder, taking the stairs two at a time, her huffing lungs glad they entered the second floor and didn't go another flight to the third.

She yelled. "I called the police." Not entirely true, but good for them to know she expected company.

Entering the second floor with its open concept, home décor stations, the person she chased had turned to confront her, pulling a gun, so she grabbed the first thing she saw. A vase, that probably cost more than she made in a day. It startled the intruder enough that the umbrella stand she snared and swung next had a chance to connect.

The person hit the floor, unconscious. But they weren't alone. A rustle of fabric drew her attention across the dim showroom to a shadow on the far side.

Before she could flee—because she'd reached the limits of her bravery—the second intruder smashed through a window to escape. Obviously, they'd watched one too many action movies. Did the fall kill or injure them? She'd paused on that sill and had no intention of jumping even before Matt yelled at her not to do it.

"Any idea who it is?" Joleen asked, drawing her back to the present as she checked the intruder for identification.

She shook her head. "No clue, but he wasn't alone. The other person got away on a bike. Mr. Arbuckle chased them."

Joleen blinked. "Arbuckle as in your client?"

She nodded.

"Why would he do that? And wait a second, how come your client was here in the first place? Was he in cahoots with them?"

She bit her lower lip. "We were having dinner at Maria's Fine Pasta when the alarm went off."

That got Joleen's attention. "That's not a place to do business."

"Their pasta is really good," was her poor defense.

"You don't need to apologize for being horny. I saw your Mr. Arbuckle. Stupid name. Hot man. I can see why you'd want to have him over for dessert."

There was no point in lying. Joleen would ferret it out with the first syllable. "He's only here for a few days."

"Sounds perfect to me. A little of bit of fun, then send him on his way. No fuss. No muss."

Funny how it sounded callous and cold when Joleen said it aloud.

"I didn't mean to get involved with him." She felt a need to explain.

"But you did. Happens to the best of us. I still remember Mrs. Robinson." Joleen smiled. "We had a great time on that yacht of hers before she lost it."

More like the feds confiscated it for crimes against the state.

"He's not even technically a client since the property he wants is actually sold."

"Then sell him another one. Or don't. What matters is that you enjoy him while you can."

"I've never had a fling before." And only a few relationships.

"The important thing to remember is no regrets. Just relax and enjoy it while it lasts. Think of it as a gift to yourself. It is, after all, almost Christmas," Joleen said, flipping over the guy to tie his wrists. "Speaking of which, the office holiday party is the day after tomorrow. You bringing him as your date? Because, if not, then I'll bet Marissa would take him." The older woman with her elegant blonde looks and svelte figure would chew him up and spit him out.

Jealousy surged hot and quick. "He's mine." Quickly corrected to, "As my client, I'll of course offer him an invite."

"Un-hunh." Joleen turned to the guy stirring on the floor. "Sleeping beauty is waking up. What do you say we ask him a few questions?"

"Do I have to watch?" Her stomach churned.

She'd never get used to this part of the business. BBI, short for Bad Boy Inc., was more than a realty office. It acted as a cover for more illicit dealings. Not that she usually had any part in them. Her daddy learned early on she didn't have the stomach for it.

"Nah. Go home. I'll let you know what I find out."

As Joleen took her prisoner, Kayla stirred, sitting up, holding her head, with a groan.

"You okay?" Blake asked. "I think someone drugged your coffee."

The night guard looked nauseous. "If they did, I never even tasted it."

"Not your fault." They'd been targeted. Again. She thought someone had been in their office the night before. There was no glitch in the security system, and despite nothing being on camera, she'd gotten the distinct impression someone had been there. But that person at least acted subtly. Today's intrusion lacked any kind of finesse.

Why the sudden interest in this building? She'd let the more devious minds figure it out. She was going home. But not on the bus. Since she'd knew she'd be drinking, she'd not brought her car. She was loading a ride sharing app when she heard the hum of an engine. A peek outside showed a motorcycle pulled to the curb. Matt straddled it, looking quite at ease despite his less than adequate coat and wind-chafed cheeks.

She stepped outside, and before she could think, she stalked close for a harangue. "You idiot. What were you thinking going after them like that?"

"I was thinking I'd do a citizen's arrest. Alas, they lost me in the maze-like streets of this city." He grimaced. "I hate one-ways."

"Teach you to steal a bike and go haring off," she grumbled.

"You okay?" he asked.

"Yes." She didn't tell him she'd whacked a guy with an umbrella stand. He might not understand.

He glanced around. "I don't see any cops."

"No point. We interrupted the intruders before they could steal anything," she lied smoothly.

"What about drugging your guard?"

"Turns out Kayla's on some serious meds for a back condition. She says she fell asleep on her own." She wondered if he bought it.

"What about the second burglar?"

"What do you mean?" she asked, clasping her hands lest he see the trembling. She hated lying.

"Don't play stupid, Blake. Two bikes. Two perps."

"I guess they ran off while I was dealing with Kayla." Would he buy her tiny little fib?

His lips flattened. "Get on."

"Excuse me?"

"Get your ass on the bike, Blake."

She eyed the sliver of seat left. "I don't think so."

"Either you get on the back and hold on tight or I'll toss you in my lap and you can watch the pavement up close. Either way you're coming with me."

"I don't like threats."

"Too bad. I can tell you're shaken."

"And how is getting on the bike supposed to help?"

"Because I'm going to take you home."

"Oh."

"Would it help if I said I'll go slow? As slow as you need," he drawled.

She shivered, but she also got on that bike. It proved to be more torture than she could have imagined, having her body wrapped tight around him, her cheek leaning on his back, arms around his torso, her thighs snuggling him.

She gave him her address. It seemed stupid not to.

Just like it seemed dumb to not say, "Want to come upstairs for a drink?"

She knew exactly where a drink would lead.

And so did he, yet he said, "Can't tonight. I've

got some work stuff to handle. I'll call you tomorrow."

CHAPTER NINE

Winters the Iceman knew he had to stay away, so he tried to work, and had a good jerk, but he didn't even last the day.

LEAVING HER KILLED HIM. HE STAYED AWAY THAT night. Then the next day. Made it just past dinner before he found himself knocking at her apartment. She opened her door but said nothing.

"Sorry I left you in the lurch last night."

"It's fine." Her words were stiff like her posture, which seemed at odds with the happy sloth riding a candy cane on her shirt.

"No, it's not." He rubbed a hand through his hair. "You weren't a complication I counted on."

"Sorry," she replied sardonically.

"It's not your fault. It's mine. I can't focus. And apparently, I can't stay away. Blake, I—"

Whatever he might have said next was halted by the sudden press of her lips. One moment she was staring at him, and the next, she was in his arms, kissing him. Dragging him inside. And he was kicking that door shut.

"Why did you leave?" she asked as she tugged at his shirt.

"Because I'm not good for you."

"So why come back?"

"Because I missed you." The stupid, honest truth.

"You barely know me."

"Trust me, I'm aware of how crazy that sounds." Aware that this woman did something to him. Made his cold heart feel again.

He stripped her bare that he might finally see her in all her naked glory. They kissed, mouths open and breath mingling. Somehow, even with their bodies pressed tight, he divested her of her clothing. He couldn't see her, but he could feel her. He let his hands travel over her smooth skin, enjoying her cries of pleasure and the way her whole body vibrated at his touch.

She tugged at his clothes, frenzied in her need, even popping a button, which was fucking sexy as hell. Once she'd stripped his shirt, she clung to him, her nude upper body rubbing against his. Making him throb something fierce.

He wanted nothing more than to sink his cock into her. To ride her as she clawed his back.

But first, he wanted to taste. Explore. He traced his way down her body with his mouth and hands, nibbling the soft skin of her neck before moving to the valley between her heavy breasts. She cried out when he took her nipple into his mouth. Uttered a strangled moan when he bit her soft flesh.

As he sucked, his cock throbbed in time, aching with need. He moved them to a couch, sat her on it that he could better play. He kneaded her breasts, pushing them together that he might play with both erect tips. When that wasn't enough, he pushed her down on the couch, and she parted her thighs, showing him the treasure he'd pleasured before.

A hand over her mound showed how hot and wet she was for him. He slid a finger into the tight heat and groaned when her hips pushed against his hand.

If he wasn't careful, he'd lose control. He fumbled for the condom in his back pocket, a clumsy idiot that ruined the mood as he tried to roll the damned thing over his thick cock.

She slid off the couch and took over, her hands smoothing the rubber over his flesh. It was more erotic than it had a right to be, especially since she didn't let go but kept stroking him. Rubbing him. Pushing him onto his back and then straddling his waist, her damp sex brushing against him. Teasing.

"I'm not going to last if you keep doing that," he admitted through gritted teeth.

"And? Technically I'm ahead of the game." She

winked then grabbed hold of him and stroked, shifting enough she could place her mouth over him.

Holy fuck.

His hips bucked. He almost came and barely held on. Managed only a hoarse, "Give me that pussy."

She didn't obey, so he took back control, manhandling her so that her sweet sex was positioned over his mouth, and he finally tasted her.

Her slick lips parted for his tongue, and she moaned as he explored her, moaned around the cock in her mouth, which meant he groaned against her quivering sex. He discovered her sensitive clit and flicked it again and again, loving how she shuddered each time. She paid him back, gripping tight, bobbing her head up and down the length of his cock. He worked her swollen nub faster, sucking and nipping, and she reacted by sucking hard. Hard enough he wished there was no condom in the way.

He could feel his body tightening. He was going to come if she kept it up.

And she didn't seem keen on stopping. He thrust two fingers into her tight sex. She quivered at his penetration and sucked him faster. He pumped her while his tongue flicked against her clit.

With a scream that vibrated around his cock

still in her mouth, she came hard, clamping down on his fingers. Pushing him over the edge.

He came. And came again an hour later, this time buried inside her. He then did something he never did.

He spent the night and woke to the sense of someone watching.

A cat. Who perched on his chest and looked less than impressed he was in Blake's bed. Until he scratched it. Then the kitty purred and rolled. It disturbed Blake, who groaned, "Too early."

He laughed. "I think your cat likes me.

"Traitor," was her grumbled reply.

"I'm going to make a coffee. Want one?"

"Mhhm," was the sleepy reply.

He found her small kitchen and made breakfast. Of a sort. No avocado. Nothing whole wheat. If he was going to spend more time here, he'd need to do a grocery run. The cat was delighted to have a new human filling her bowl with something that smelled strongly of fish.

He'd never owned a pet before. Never saw the point but had to admit the feline was cute and friendly. She chose to ignore her food to rub against the hand that fed her. The fur silky soft. He trailed his digits along it, and the cat abruptly flung herself onto her back, exposing her belly.

The fur proved even softer underneath, and as

he rubbed, the feline began to purr, a little machine that rumbled and stretched.

Until she suddenly grabbed him with all four paws and teeth!

Lightly, though. Not enough to truly prick the skin, still purring. Was it playing? Or just psychotic? Either way, it was entertaining. Maybe he should think of getting one when he slowed down with work.

Slow down? Now there was something he didn't think of often, mostly because during his down time he quickly got bored. What else was there to do other than plan the next job? His attention strayed in the direction of where he'd left Blake. He could think of things he'd enjoy doing if he had the right person.

On the way back to the bedroom with coffee, he noticed the lack of holiday décor. No tree or lights. Just a porcelain snowman, who looked old, sitting on the table by her door. Odd for a woman with so many Christmas sweaters.

As he entered the bedroom, he murmured, "Rise and shine."

She rolled and stretched, blinking at him through heavy eyelids. "Do I have to?" Her voice emerged husky.

Sexy.

Distracting.

He thrust a coffee at her. “Made you something.”

She eyed the blackness and then him. “Please tell me it at least has sugar.”

“Let me guess, you want cream too?”

She nodded. By the time he returned with the syrupy mess, she was sitting in her bed, sheet pooled around her waist. A goddess that made him want to forget his job and spend the day here, with her.

“Despite your many sweaters, you seem to be lacking a Christmas tree.”

“I skipped one this year. Not much point in having one just for myself.” She said it as if it were okay, yet he got the sense it wasn’t.

“I don’t think I’ve ever had one.”

“Even as a kid?”

“I didn’t have a great childhood.” He frowned. That was more than he usually admitted.

“I’m sorry.”

“Why?”

“Because some of my best memories are around the Christmases I spent with my family.”

“I don’t need presents.”

“It’s about more than gifts,” she stated, leaning back with her mug held in two hands. “It’s that warm and fuzzy feeling you get from spending time with people you love.”

“Are you sure that’s not the spiked eggnog?”

She snickered. "Only when we used to let Aunt Jean make it."

He wanted to know more about this Aunt Jean and all the things that made Blake who she was.

Instead he leaned in for a kiss and muttered, "I've got to hit my hotel for a change of clothes. I have business to attend to this morning."

"Okay." She sipped her coffee.

Just okay? His pathetic ass then said, "Meet me for lunch?"

"I'd love that," she said with a beaming smile.

They had lunch. Then sex at his hotel. Then went to see a house she thought he might like. Had sex again.

He was beginning to wonder if he'd ever tire of her. Each time was as intense as the last.

Then it happened, the thing he'd been working toward.

She asked him after dessert while they were sprawled naked on the couch, their limbs entwined. "Are you busy tomorrow night?"

"Why?" he asked.

"I don't suppose you want to be my date for the office Christmas party?"

He only felt a slight twinge of guilt as he said, "I'd love to."

CHAPTER TEN

There's no place like home for the holidays; unless it's in bed with my lover.

Why had she invited him? She hadn't meant to, but it slipped out. Now she was nervous. Stupid, yet she couldn't help it. She'd only rarely introduced men she dated to her father and friends. In this case, the term boyfriend didn't even apply to Matt. The blunt truth? *I'm bringing my lover to a work function.* Never thought she'd have the opportunity to say that. Women with lovers were glamorous or rich, not full-hipped with baggage—and an over-protective dad.

That Matt had chosen her still felt a touch surreal, even if she had the beard rub marks on her breasts to prove it. It chafed, but in a good way. However, the pinkness made her glad her outfit for the night lacked a plunging neckline.

Matt had left a few hours ago, after giving her a

long kiss, to get ready at his hotel. A good thing since she needed time to prep herself.

She did a full shave. And she meant full. She would probably regret that in a few days, but this was a special occasion. Her last night perhaps before he left. Because she assumed he'd leave before Christmas, and the Eve would hit shortly.

Pathetic to hope he'd stay a few more days? More like sad to realize the amazing whirlwind tryst might soon come to an end. Better make each moment count.

She dressed with extra care, glad she'd splurged on the matching undergarments and the stay-up stockings. As for her party dress?

When Matt arrived to pick her up, his eyeballs almost fell out. "You can't be seriously thinking of going out wearing that?"

"Do you like?" she asked, twirling for him. The navy blue knit sweater dress hugged her curves. She'd bought it before putting on those ten extra pounds. It fit more snuggly than she usually preferred; however, his eyes weren't on her hips or tits but the image painstakingly sewn over the course of weeks. The main parts were done in felt then decorated with a few buttons, some fringe, a bit of glitter. The twigs she'd picked during a walk

"It's definitely original?" was his hesitant reply.

She glanced down at her dress, decorated with a giant snowman wearing a top hat, actual buttons for its eyes, a pompon for its nose, and a scarf that fluttered. She'd matched it with a belt that had twinkling lights.

"I made it myself," she said, still grinning. "Check this out." She pressed a rhinestone button, and a tinny version of "Jingle Bells" began to play while LED lights, woven back and forth across her masterpiece, blinked in rhythm.

"That is unbelievable." Disbelief tugged his features.

She couldn't hold in her laughter. "Isn't it just hideous?"

"You know it's ugly?" he asked tentatively.

"On purpose. Ugly sweaters, and outfits, are actually a tradition in my family. We were doing it before it became fashionable. My mom started it."

"Your mother has an odd sense of humor."

"My mother's dead."

"Oh fuck."

She shook her head. "It happened a long time ago. Home invasion." She shrugged and then quickly continued to speak before he could say something that would ruin her makeup. "After she died, my dad thought we should keep doing it as an homage to her. We're sure she's watching us from heaven, laughing, wearing her own hideous creation." Her smile must have held some sadness in it, because he moved close for a hug.

"I'm sorry. I didn't realize."

And she'd done it. Ruined their happy moment. "How could you know?" she said lightly, suddenly reminded that for all they'd been intimate, in many respects, they didn't know each other. "It's not something I advertise. And since the whole ugly-sweater thing became popular, most people don't think anything of it."

"I don't care if it's the latest trend. That dress is a travesty to snowmen everywhere." His lips twisted, and his tone was wry.

"Would it help if I said I wore snowman undies and matching bra?"

That got him to laugh. "Now I want to undress you even more."

The man was always in the mood to strip her. Bare her. Love every inch of her body until she screamed. He wasn't selfish one bit in bed. On the contrary, he liked to make her come first with his mouth or fingers and then a second time when he was inside her.

"There's only one more thing left to complete my outfit," she declared. "Can you guess what it is?"

"I'm afraid to find out," he said with a twitch of his lips.

"I have a matching tie." At the time she'd made the dress, she'd been dating someone. It didn't last. Hence the ten pounds.

"A tie?" he repeated as if it made little sense to him.

She grabbed it from the chair she'd draped it over. It had a googly-eyed snowman on it, wrapped in a garland of light—rhinestones that glittered if the light caught them.

"You want me to wear that?" Incredulous didn't even describe it.

"It was all I could manage on short notice." A pity they'd not met sooner. She'd seen an epic red Christmas suit, the jacket sewn with red sequins that shimmered green when ruffled. "Will you wear it?"

"I can't believe I'm going to agree." He removed his dark and somber neckwear, and for a moment, she was tempted to start undoing all those buttons and kissing the flesh she uncovered.

But then that would lead to her messing up her hair, plus them being late. It wouldn't set a good note with her father, who had actually called her that afternoon, asking why she'd not been in the office. Then he casually asked about their latest client.

"Have you sold that Arbuckle a house yet?" he'd asked. "You've been out of the office meeting with him rather often."

"We're still looking." She didn't mention the fact they spent much of that time naked in her apartment.

"Hopefully you'll find something for him soon. When does he leave?"

"I'm not sure. He hasn't said."

"You should bring him to the party. It's about time I meet him."

Why? Had her father been talking to Joleen? Did Daddy know she and Matt were seeing each other? He better not because that would mean he was watching her too closely again. She'd snapped when she discovered his surveillance during college. He'd claimed it was for her own good. They'd compromised with her agreeing to a state-of-the-art security system.

She was being paranoid. If her father thought for a moment she was involved with a client, he would have shown up at her apartment, baseball bat in hand.

She'd invited him, and Matt had immediately said yes. The fact her father told her to do it after the fact meant it wouldn't look odd. Them showing up in matching outfits? People were bound to notice.

Let them. She wasn't ashamed of being a woman. Of having needs. She could do worse than have people judging her for sleeping with a hot guy.

As Matt looped the tie to perfection, she couldn't help but feel a pang of sadness. This whirlwind past few days had been perfect.

She leaned up and kissed him. Soft and sweet.

Turning hot and passionate.

"Maybe we should forget the party," she murmured.

"Won't your father notice?"

She wrinkled her nose as her ardor cooled. "Yes, and that probably isn't a good thing."

The last time she'd not checked in when expected, her father had shown up at her shortly lived yoga class. She only needed to land on her chin once to realize it wasn't for her, and given her daddy was partially to blame, she refused to talk to him for a whole week after.

Helping her into her coat, Matt asked, "So where are we going? Restaurant? Bar? Boss's living room?"

She'd only been told the actual location that morning. The company had changed the venue a few times, along with the date. The owner of this BBI office—which had franchises all over the world—took paranoia to a new level. Then again, given what BBI was involved in, not really a surprise. Worldwide luxury realty was the cover for Bad Boy Inc., an agency of mercenaries that committed crimes for money. Although, it should be noted, they did have some lines they wouldn't cross. Killing wasn't one of them. But children were off the list. Bad Boy operated in shadows where concealment was key. They couldn't afford to be outed, not with the enemies they'd made over the years.

"We're going to the Grizzly Lake Chalet." There was a certain irony in the fact the Christmas party was being held in the same house where she and Matt first made out.

He arched a brow. "A sale property being used for your office party?"

"Sold property," she corrected. "The deal was completed yesterday morning."

"And as a thank-you, the seller offered it up to celebrate?

"Actually, the new buyer did. He insisted on a quick possession."

"Money talks," he murmured. "Nice of the new owner to throw your company a Christmas party as a thank-you."

"Not that strange. He and his wife are friends with quite a few of us in the BBI family."

Ariel—formerly known as Meredith, code name Cougar Mom—was a woman with fiery red locks and a tendency of mothering Blake. Ariel had dated her father for a bit after a project they worked on. She also more recently had been in town setting up the interior decorating office on the first floor of their building while her husband got the newest BBI office up and running.

"And who is this mysterious host?"

No point in hiding it anymore. "Hugo Laurentian."

He whistled. "I've heard of him. Reclusive billionaire."

"But nice guy. He and my dad have been friends for a long time." She used to call him uncle when she was younger.

"We should get going." He offered his arm, and she tucked her hand in it.

The moment felt like one of those holiday specials. It just lacked the music and the perfect kiss in light falling snow under mistletoe.

In her case, she could probably expect the disaster that made the heroine cry.

While she'd offered to drive, he'd stated it was his turn and promised to not have a single drink so she could enjoy herself.

He'd rented a sedan, the front leather seats wide and the leg room plenty. Nicely scented. Clean. The leather warm on her butt. Light jazz playing.

"What do you think?" he asked.

"It's nicer than my apartment. I could live in here comfortably." She stroked the buttery seat covering.

"I know something else you can pet."

Crude, but she laughed. He knew how to amuse her. She was going to miss him when he left.

"What's the sad face for?" He always seemed to be paying attention to her. More than anyone ever had. Unless her father counted.

"Nothing."

"Blake." His voice had a warning tone.

So she said the one thing guaranteed to shut him up. The thing that sent men packing. "I know I said no strings and all, but..." She bit her lip. "I hate that you have to go. I'm going to miss you."

A silence followed her words before his low reply. "To my surprise, I'm going to miss you as well. Enough that I am thinking of extending my trip."

"Really?" She turned a startled gaze on him.

His lips crooked. "Being with you is more enjoyable than I would have imagined. You don't bore me."

"Gee, thanks."

A short-barked laugh emerged from him. "It's not an insult but a huge compliment. I'm not a people person."

"Says the man who charmed my panties off almost the first day."

"When I'm around you, I'm a different kind of man."

"As opposed to..."

"Anyone who truly knows me wouldn't call me nice or charming."

"What do they call you then?"

"Death."

"What?" she said, startled at his muttered reply.

"People who know me would say I'm ruthless. I don't let anything get in my way."

"What's wrong with that?"

"Not everyone is happy with the end result."

"You can't please everyone. Only do your best."

He coughed.

"You okay?"

"Yeah, but we got off topic. You were saying you didn't want me to go."

Her cheeks heated. "Meaning I'll miss you." But she refused to beg. She had to have some limits with this man.

"I don't know if I'm ready to let you go."

"Oh." The statement pleased her. "Things have really changed since we first met."

"No kidding." His hand slid down to the hem of her dress and began dragging it up her thigh.

"I guess it's a good thing that, instead of wanting to smack you, I want to sleep with you." She boldly put her hand over his groin. Already hard. For her.

"As if we sleep," he said on a snicker.

"Good point. I doubt the neighbors are either given the screaming." She squeezed.

He growled. "Don't make me pull this car over and see if those panties really do have snowmen."

"Wanna see?" She pulled her dress up and showed him. He took his gaze off the road, and the car swerved.

"Fuck. Put that away. We can't."

"Why not?" she said, grabbing his hand and

wantonly placing it where she wanted him to touch her.

"Because I doubt you want to walk into your office party looking as if you've just been royally fucked."

She sighed. "Good point. I guess, worst case, I could just go the bathroom and take care of myself."

"You are an evil woman, Blake Jenners. So very, very evil."

She laughed, whereas he made a noise that only made her feel more womanly and powerful. He loved her curves. He seemed to also enjoy her mind. She blossomed in his presence, and he wanted to stick around to spend more time with her.

Merry Christmas to me.

She felt blessed as they parked alongside the other cars, luxury vehicles for the most part. The BBI office party would draw a crowd from near and far. Why rent a mundane sedan when they could have something posh? BBI dealt in luxury, and it never hurt to play that part.

The house was lit up. Clear Christmas lights rimmed the roof line and wrapped around the posts holding up the portico. The windows blinked with more Christmas cheer. Even the trees lining the drive were draped in merry apparel.

The only thing out of place? An inflatable

snowman that had fallen over in front of a Santa. Given the stiff breeze, they appeared to be doing a sexual act.

She snickered.

Whereas Matt grumbled, "Not funny." He was so unamused he stalked over and righted the snowman then punched Santa in the gut.

Which only made her laugh harder. As he came back toward her, she couldn't help but exclaim, "What did Santa ever do to you?"

"I'm not a fan," he said, sliding his arm around her.

"I think you have a thing for snowmen."

"Can you blame me given you're wearing that dress? I can't wait to see those panties again."

Those panties might not survive if they got any wetter. She appreciated his firm grip as they traversed the drive, slippery in spots as a light snow covered the land.

Funny how she never fell when she was with him.

"Think your ass mark is still on the window?" he asked as they hit the first step.

"Matt!" she squeaked, her foot slipping.

His arm tightened. "Gotcha."

She smiled. Nice to know she could trust him to not let her down.

As they approached the front door, everything was the same, even the welcome mat. Hugo had bought the chalet fully furnished. Even insisted on keeping the decorations. It made using it as a vacation property simpler. As to how Ariel managed to cook on short notice?

She didn't. The party was being catered. To the side of the house, Blake noticed two vans with matching company logos parked close to the side door kitchen entrance.

Before she could knock, the door swung open, and a glossy-eyed Joleen beamed at her. "About time you showed. Everyone is here already, getting their merry on."

The party appeared to be in full swing. Christmas music played from embedded speakers. Staff in elf costumes served, handling the large trays with an ease she'd never manage. People milled about in the great room, voices rising in a cacophony of sound. Just about everyone had a drink in hand.

"Give me your coat." Joleen waggled her fingers.

After she'd shed her outerwear and boots, Matt kept her steady as she slipped on her shoes. He then handed over his own overcoat and removed the snow rubbers from his loafers.

Joleen waggled a glass in front of her. "Try the eggnog. It is freaking good. And the food!" Her workmate kissed the tips of her fingers.

"How many nogs have you had?" Blake asked as Joleen weaved in place.

"Just two plus this one. Why?" She blinked a few more times than necessary.

Blake frowned. She'd steer clear of it given it appeared to be a little more alcohol laden than she enjoyed.

With Matt's fingers lightly touching her back, they entered the great room. Given it was evening, the Christmas tree was lit, the recessed lighting in the room soft. The windows reflected the room and the twenty or so people milling. Many of them familiar faces, such as Kayla, recovered from her attack. Nestor, the other guard Kayla swapped shifts with. But she also saw a few clients in the crowd. Wealthy people who kept the legit side of BBI flush with cash.

The drink trays circulated—eggnog, wine, frothy-looking ice shots. While they both took a glass, she noticed Matt set his down right away, keeping his word about not drinking. She had only a tiny sip. Creamy and delicious. Didn't taste spiked. Maybe Joleen had added a little something.

More than a few people in attendance had made an effort to add a holiday theme to their outfit. Meredith stood by the fireplace—oops, she had to think of her as Ariel now. She wore a snowflake dress of light blue edged in lace. Her contribution to the ugly Christmas outfit. She carried it off with elegance, as did her husband in his matching light blue suit, patterned with silver filigree snowflakes, and a silver tie.

"There's Hugo and his wife, Ariel," she said, pointing. Since the eggnog tasted fine, she drank another mouthful.

"About time you showed up," boomed her father as he approached them from behind.

They pivoted to say hello. Her lips widened in a smile as she beheld her father in full Santa gear—if the jolly red fellow had a fetish for Elvis. Right down to the red suede shoes.

"When did you get that?" she asked. "It is atrocious and amazing."

Only he didn't return her smile. He wasn't looking at her at all. Rather his gaze narrowed in on Matt. "What the fuck are *you* doing here?" growled her dad.

"You told me to invite him," she said in confusion, putting down her glass.

"This is your Arbuckle?" her father huffed, whipping to glance at her for a second.

"Yes. Why are you so mad? You told me to bring him to the party."

"I told you to bring a client with you, not this imposter." Her father glared at Matt.

"Are you still going on about that?" drawled a voice she knew but with a tone and expression she didn't recognize. Matt appeared carved of uncompromising stone. No hint of the lover or the charming man she'd gotten to know.

Blake peeked at her still scowling father. "You two know each other." Stated, not asked.

"In a sense. We met on a job." Matt's voice held cold amusement.

"Met? You stole that commission from me."

"Not my fault you were too slow."

"I set up that entire deal, and you swooped in and stole it out from under me." Her dad snorted. "What are you doing with my daughter?"

"He's looking for a house," she said, stepping in, worry nagging at her. Was this about a real estate deal gone bad? It seemed a little extreme, but the alternative just couldn't be possible.

"Like fuck he's here house shopping," snapped her father. "Exactly what are you up to, Winters?"

Winters? She glanced at her lover.

His expression remained flat. "Working. What about you? Don't tell me you left the business to sell houses."

Her father arched a brow. "A man has to make a living somehow. Especially when he has a family."

The facts kept colliding. Her head spun as she did her best to ignore what it meant. It helped that Hugo and Ariel wandered close.

"Hello, I don't think we've met." Hugo held out his hand. "Hugo Laurentian."

For a moment, Matt glanced at her, his expression frozen then grim as he turned to greet their host. “Hello, I’m Mathias Winters.”

Wait, what? She blinked.

Someone muttered, “Holy shit. I thought I recognized him from that job in Panama. It’s the Iceman.”

“Mr. Winters. I’ve heard of you. Why are you here?” Hugo asked.

“I was asked to hand deliver a present to you.”

Her father, Blake Sr., blustered, “Since when are you an errand boy?”

“When the price is right.” Matt’s hand dropped to his pocket, and she could tell the BBI folk from the clients brought to wine and dazzle. The BBI people slid hands into jackets, the ladies tensed, no one relaxed when Matt held out a box that he pulled from his pocket.

On a positive note, no one shot him. Not in front of outsiders. They wouldn’t act unless the threat was clearly visible.

Hugo didn’t accept it. He eyed Matt-Arbuckle-Winters. “I don’t accept gifts from strangers.”

“Then don’t. I was told to deliver it.”

“And Hugo has refused. Leave or I’ll make you leave,” threatened her father.

“How long are you going to hold a grudge about what happened in the past?” Matt asked, his tone an exasperated sigh. “Yes, I took out your target.”

“You didn’t just take him out. You destroyed all

the evidence we needed to shut down his operation," Blake Sr. railed.

"Wait a second, you're *that* Winters? The one he's always complaining about?" Joleen chuckled, but her amusement died as she glanced at Blake, the woman betrayed.

The truth slapped her hard as she finally put all the pieces together. Matt was a mercenary for hire like her father. She glanced at the present he still held. "You used me to get close to Hugo."

He didn't need to say a word. She saw it in his face.

She slapped him before stalking away.

CHAPTER ELEVEN

He led her to the attic he found and took her by a rack. He might have fucked her hard again, if someone hadn't bloody attacked.

THE LOOK OF BETRAYAL ON BLAKE'S FACE JUST about killed Mathias. He'd never meant to hurt her. Never meant to fall for her. Definitely never expected she'd find out the truth in such a brutal fashion.

It didn't help that her daddy—a man Mathias knew as Roarke—smirked. If Mathias weren't convinced he'd wind up Swiss-cheesed, he'd have punched him. Then again, he couldn't exactly blame Roarke. Matt had been sleeping with his daughter.

"Who gave you the package?"

The question distracted him from the fleeing Blake. He turned to see Hugo's wife eying him, a wine glass held between two fingers. She seemed familiar, and drunk. She swayed in her high heels.

"Have we met?"

She smiled. "I'm flattered you remember. It's been awhile."

The moment she confirmed, he remembered. "What was it, ten years ago? With that guy in Colombia." The one who died in a freak accident before Mathias could kill him.

"Martinez learned the hard way to respect broken glass. It can be so dangerous." She waggled hers, but it didn't slosh, the wine in the bottom less than a mouthful.

He realized the circle around them had widened, with some people ushered to other parts of the room, separating the innocent sheep from the wolves, drinks and food being shoved at them.

"Let's cut the bullshit. I'm not here to cause trouble," Mathias said, spreading his hands.

"Then what's that?" Roarke asked, pointing to the box Mathias still clutched.

"A watch."

"You opened it?" Hugo asked, only a slight twitch of a brow showing his surprise.

"Someone wants to pay me a hundred grand to deliver something, fuck yeah I'm taking a peek."

"A hundred?" Joleen, the woman he'd met at the door, whistled. "Fuck, for that price I wouldn't have cared if it held a bomb."

"Who gave it to you?" Hugo asked.

Mathias shrugged. "Don't know." Even if he did,

he wouldn't tell. People who ratted out clients didn't work for long in the business.

"Open it," Hugo asked, even as his wife cast him a startled glance.

"Okay." He tugged the ribbon then opened the hinged lid, revealing the old watch.

"I don't recognize it." Not a single expression creased Hugo's face, yet Mathias would have sworn the man was lying.

"Doesn't really matter. It's yours. Keep it. Toss it. Up to you." He placed it on a passing tray and grabbed a canape, something squishy and pink on a cracker.

"What use do I have for an old broken watch?" Hugo muttered, turning away. "Let's dance," he said to his wife, never realizing he'd revealed something.

Mathias had never told him the watch was broken.

Not his problem.

Roarke chose to remain and glowered. "You going to leave now that you've delivered your package?"

"Leave? But the party is just starting." He grabbed a glass of nog and raised it, pretending to take a sip. The glazed expressions on a few faces spoke to the liberal imbibing of it.

"What's your game, Iceman?"

"No game. I've done my job. I am off the clock

as they say. Ready to enjoy the delights of your quaint town." He deliberately baited the other man.

Roarke growled. "Leave my daughter alone."

"Too late for that."

He expected Roarke to snap. He was wrong.

The man laughed. "You won't be dallying with my girl anymore, not now that she knows the truth. Tell me, did you like the present I left you out front?"

The snowman and Santa, one of them getting fucked.

"You knew I was here," he huffed.

Roarke grinned so wide his face almost split. "Not at first. Your Arbuckle cover was quite clever, but I happened to see you on a security camera."

"And didn't have me taken out?" Surprising given where he'd spent the last few nights.

"That would have been my preference, but I needed you away from my daughter first."

"Is this where you tell me to step outside so you can kill me?"

Roarke shook his head. "Hugo said I can't take you out unless you do something stupid first. Apparently messing with my daughter isn't enough."

"I have the utmost admiration for her." He felt a need to let her father know he wasn't just using her. "She's beautiful and brilliant. In other circumstances..." He trailed off because he didn't know what he'd do.

"There will never be a circumstance where I'd want her dating you. Go home, Winters. There's nothing here for you."

Roarke seemed sure, but Mathias remained unconvinced.

He eyed the stairs where he'd seen her climb. She obviously didn't want to see him.

He should leave. This was her party.

Instead, he stood to the side, indulging in idle chitchat with a few agents more curious than aggressive. One chap, a hulking fellow by the name of Gerome, asked him if he'd be interested in perhaps working full-time for one employer.

An intriguing idea, especially once he heard who Gerome worked for.

He barely moved, and never out of sight of the staircase. He knew from their walkthrough that there was no other way down to the main floor, unless she went out a window. He highly doubted she'd ever be that desperate.

A few minutes passed. Thirty. Blake remained missing. He watched as her father, then Joleen, even their hostess, went upstairs to talk with her, only to return without her.

She probably felt betrayed and with good reason.

Guilt wasn't something he was accustomed to,

and neither was that heavy feeling in his gut. The one that seemed to think he should apologize.

She doesn't want to hear it.

Or was he too afraid to tell her he'd done wrong?

The waiter came by, trying to force him to take a glass of nog or punch. He waved his still full vessel. Not so the rest of the party. Even Hugo's man, Gerome, looked a little bleary-eyed.

He should leave. Go home to an empty house. An empty life.

But if he stayed, he'd have to find his balls, apologize, and see if he could salvage something.

Either way he had to stop stalling.

He set his glass down and went up the stairs, certain he'd hear Roarke challenge him when he realized what he was doing. But the man was currently singing along to "Rudolph" and not paying him any attention. No one stopped him from reaching the second floor of the house.

He glanced to his left and the double doors at the far end. He doubted she'd be in the master bedroom. To his right, more bedrooms. He checked the closest one done in shades of plaid. It was empty.

The next had some kind of springtime flowery theme. Also vacant. The third room was a study, lined with books and a comfortable chair. There was a set of spiral stairs in the corner leading to the attic room tucked into the very peak of the house. A craft room with bars dangling rolls of paper, spindles of ribbon, and a veritable vomit of Christmas cheer and bows. In the middle was a counter with drawers, probably full of more useless crap.

None of it mattered when he beheld the rounded shoulders of a woman betrayed. She hugged herself as she stared out of the window.

"Blake..." he said softly.

She stiffened. "Go away."

"We need to talk."

"No, we don't. I'm not interested in anything you have to say."

"Well, that's too bad because I'm going to speak and you're going to listen."

She whirled, eyes flashing with anger. "Listen to what? More lies? We both know you're good at that. You used me. Seduced me because of a job." Her chest heaved with her agitation. Cheeks red with fury. Still beautiful. It hurt him to see the betrayal in her gaze.

"I'll admit that was my plan at first." He stuck to the truth and deserved the stinging slap. His face turned with the impact, but the blow to his heart was more painful.

"You asshole!"

When she would have slapped him again, he grabbed her wrists and pulled her into him. "Yes, I'm an asshole. A cold-hearted bastard. I admit I set out to use you to complete my mission. But there is one thing I didn't lie about and that's how I feel about you."

"Is knowing you're horny for me supposed to help?" she asked on an incredulous note.

"This isn't about sex. I care for you."

"Not enough to tell me the truth." Her voice thickened.

"And how was I supposed to explain? Hey, Blake, FYI, I'm a killer for hire."

"You lied to me about everything."

"Not true. I told you my real name. Matt. Short for Mathias."

She glared. "Not helping."

"You can't throw all the blame on me. You're not completely innocent in this. You're Roarke's daughter. The guy who can whisper any lock open. Who managed to steal that painting out from under the most sophisticated security system. I'm going to wager BBI is a cover for his activities, meaning you obviously do more than just realty."

For a moment she looked like she'd say one thing, only to slump. "Mostly right except for the part where I'm involved. I'm one hundred percent legit and boring. While most of the office is gallivanting around, handling big property deals"—she crooked her fingers in air quotes—"I'm making sure the paperwork is filed, keeping everything on the straight and narrow so they don't draw attention."

"You've done a brilliant job," he admitted. While he'd noticed oddities, his interest in Blake made him neglect looking any deeper.

"Congrats on knowing the secret."

"Blake." He rubbed a hand through his hair, not knowing the right words to say.

"Why haven't you left? You did what you came for."

"I meant what I said earlier. I don't want to leave. You," he added in case that wasn't clear.

"Still got another part to your mission?"

He shook his head. "No work. I'd like to spend more time with you."

Her chin dropped. "I can't trust you."

The words shattered his icy heart. "Fuck." He couldn't apologize enough, so he instead snared her around the waist and drew her close for a kiss.

Her mouth trembled, and he held still. If she pushed him away... If she said no...

To his relief she kissed him back, grabbing him with a franticness that had him groaning.

He could fix this. Make things right. Show her that not everything was a lie.

He sat her on that island, shoving aside the paper and scissors atop it. Her lips were parted. Her eyes bright.

He put a hand on her knee and slid it up her leg, snaring her dress and pushing it to the top of her thighs. She parted them and leaned back, braced on her hands.

The crotch of her panties peeked, the snowmen on them distracting. The fabric was damp when he pressed the darker ones. She was always so wet when he touched her. Desired him as ardently as he needed her.

He pivoted her until she could lie lengthwise, and then he grabbed her legs and dragged her so that when he bent forward, he could bury his face against her pubes. Her bare mound.

He glanced at her. "You didn't have to do that."

"Enjoy it while you can because I doubt I'll do it again," she murmured.

He nuzzled the shaven area before he shifted lower and found her clit. The moment he latched on, she bucked. Her hips thrust against his mouth. He held her steady as he licked and sucked. His tongue probed between her nether lips, lapping at her honey.

She moaned, her head back, wanton and ready.

He stood and unzipped, rolled on a condom before sliding her to the edge of that island. The head of his cock rubbed against her hot, wet sex. A hand on each hip, he yanked her onto his dick, penetrating her plump lips, feeling her channel squeezing him.

"Matt," she sighed as he took his time, slowly thrusting and grinding, driving deep and striking that sweet spot inside that always made her tighten. He pumped her, and she welcomed the thrusts of his cock, her legs wrapped around him, panting as their flesh slapped together.

Pleasure coiled tight in him, and he wanted to let go but not until she came. He altered his angle slightly and pushed her over the edge. She gasped and went taut, her body bowing as he slammed one last time, deep inside. Came.

For a moment, everything was still. Then he was pulling her into his arms, bodies still joined. He held her and buried his face in her hair, unsure for the first time of what he wanted out of life, other than the fact he wanted more of this. More of Blake.

But she was done.

She shoved at him. “Thank you for that goodbye.”

“What?” He felt as if he were partially asleep as she shoved at him and slid off the table.

“We both knew when we started sleeping together it was only temporary. You’ve done your business. Time for you to go home.”

“I don’t want to leave.”

“Then don’t. But don’t stay because of me. We’re done.”

She left, and the world became an even colder, lonelier place.

CHAPTER TWELVE

Blue Christmas; she finally understood the song even as she wondered, since when did she need a man.

As she left him in the attic, she held her chin high but inside called herself all kinds of stupid. The sexiest man she'd ever had the pleasure of knowing intimately and she was walking away.

Did she have a choice? He'd used her.

He'd also apologized.

He was a killer.

Just like her dad. Something she tried to not think about. Too late. The reminder thrust her into the past, and she barely managed to make it into a bathroom off the hall before the memory hit.

The dinosaur looked bright and pretty on the page. Pink with purple. No yucky green. The little girl coloring at the dining room table happily scribbled when the door to their house was kicked in. It slammed hard into the wall. She startled, sending her crayon streaking out of the lines.

Her mother, standing at the kitchen sink, turned, eyes wide. Her voice quavered as she barked at Blake, "Run to the Andersons' house. Through the back door, quick."

Blake wanted to; she just couldn't. She was frozen in place. She'd never seen her mother scared, and it frightened her. Especially when the three men in masks poured into the kitchen pointing guns.

The biggest one yelled, "Grab the woman and the kid."

Her mother screamed, "Don't you touch her!"

Fat, hot tears rolled down Blake's cheeks as her mother fought them. Her arms and legs spun like the action heroes on television. But on TV, the heroes got up when knocked to the floor and her daddy told her the red stuff was just ketchup.

She didn't think her mother had ketchup coming out of her nose.

The bad men dragged her mother to a chair and tied her to it. Then they took hold of Blake and bound her tight, too. Although one did protest, "She's just a little girl."

"Let's see how much she's worth," was the sneered response.

Then everything blurred. She remembered there was a lot of yelling and crying, some by her, as those men questioned her mother, asking about guns and drugs. When hitting her didn't give them answers, they slapped Blake. She was so shocked she couldn't cry.

But her mother snapped, flinging herself and the chair forward to smash into one of their attackers. In the strug-

gle, the knife they'd threatened with ended up shoved into her mother.

Mama, the one to read bedtime stories and kiss her gently on the forehead each night, slumped to the floor. Eyes wide open.

Gone.

Only then did Blake begin to bawl. Bawled so loud none of them ever heard her father coming home.

They didn't even realize he'd started killing them since her hiccupping sobs covered the soft pops as he aimed a gun and shot the bad men.

Killed them but could do nothing to fix her mother. Only hold Blake as she snotted on his shoulder, gulping tears and hugging him tight.

That day her innocence was stripped. Her father didn't hide what he was from her, mostly because he used it to help her when the nightmares woke her screaming. Each time, he'd rock her as long as it took to calm her, murmuring, "Shh, baby girl. Daddy's here. I'll never let anyone hurt you."

And he kept that promise. No surprise that after the home invasion he became a little overprotective. No one hurt Blake and got away with it, but even he couldn't shield her from a broken heart.

She'd screwed up so badly. Not because she'd slept with a mercenary but because she'd made the mistake of falling for one.

It was best she walked away, even as part of her wanted to go running back and say to hell with it.

The pleasure was like a drug. She wanted more, even though she knew it was bad for her.

She ran the water and washed her face, patting her hot cheeks to try and cool the heat in them. Tried to dampen the emotion.

How could one guy cause so much turmoil in such a short time? Time to forget him. To get on with her life. She needed more of that spiked eggnog. Lots more. And maybe some Christmas karaoke because she could use some happy jingle bells in her life right about now.

CHAPTER THIRTEEN

Into the laundry shaft, with a fishing wire in his hand, scooting here and there, moving with great care, taking out the enemy where he can.

MATHIAS WAITED A GOOD TEN MINUTES TO SEE IF she'd return. Pathetic.

Just like he was too cowardly to go after her and try to change her mind.

Eventually, he started down the spiral staircase. A sudden pop stopped him in his tracks.

Champagne?

Judging by the strangled scream and the shouted, "Hands up, mother fuckers," it appeared to be more ominous.

Someone had attacked the party. For real, or was this some kind of joke?

Quietly, he crept down the spiral stairs and then even more slowly down the hall until he reached the railing overlooking the great room. The guests were currently being held hostage by the staff, still dressed in their elf costumes, four of whom held automatic rifles. The guests were gathered around the tree, some of them slumped. A few were weaving where they stood. Only a couple didn't appear drunk.

Or should he say drugged? He'd thought people seemed a little more tipsy than normal, but he'd been distracted by Blake. Speaking of whom, he didn't see her among the guests. He heard the faint flush of a toilet then running water. He glanced up the hall then sprinted as quietly as he could. The moment the guest bathroom door opened, he swept her into his arms, a hand over her mouth as he pulled her back into the bathroom.

Her eyes flashed in anger.

He shook his head and mouthed, "Attack."

She frowned and mumbled something against his hand.

He whispered a reply. "The waiters have guns and have rounded up everyone at the party."

"My dad?" Her lips trembled.

"No one seems to have been shot. But I think the drinks were spiked."

"That would explain why two sips had me a little lightheaded. What do they want?"

He shrugged. "No idea. For the moment, they appear to be holding them hostage. Given there's a lot of wealthy people downstairs, I'm going to guess robbery."

"A home invasion." She sounded absolutely terrified. "We have to call for help."

She pulled out her phone from a pocket in her snowman's belly. Frowned. "No signal."

A quick check of his own device also showed a no-service sign.

"What are we going to do?" she huffed, panic making her breath fast.

"We?" A second ago she'd never wanted to see him again, and now she expected him to come to her rescue. The Iceman would tell her to solve her own problem or negotiate a price.

But in this moment, he was Mathias, the man who'd fallen for the woman with the never-ending sweaters. He wasn't cut out to be a hero, and yet she needed one. "I'll need a weapon."

"Don't you have a gun?"

"Two, actually. Both are in the car," he admitted, trying to ignore the hot shame. What kind of assassin didn't have a weapon on his body? A distracted one with the blood in his dick instead of his head.

She blinked. "You don't have a single weapon?"

"I wasn't expecting shit to hit the fan at an office party. Your boss, Hugo, is known to travel with a bodyguard. I expected to be frisked coming in the door." Only an idiot would have shown up armed, so he'd left his toys in the car. Why not? The Christmas party provided the public venue he needed to hand over the gift and hopefully get away clean. Rich people didn't need the unsavory attention of cops or the media.

"Maybe we can find one somewhere."

"What do you mean, find one? Your father is Roarke, a known knife master. As his daughter, shouldn't you always be armed?"

"I am not a fan of violence." Her nose wrinkled.

"Do you know how to fight?"

Her shoulders rolled. "You've seen my body. It was made for lounging, not fighting.

Indeed, it was. Soft and sweet the way he liked it. And also in danger. Since he only had himself to count on, he'd have to be clever. He also needed to focus without worrying about her.

"Stay here," he ordered.

"What are you going to do?"

"Prove I wasn't lying when I said I cared for you."

"By what, going out there and getting yourself killed?"

"Would you actually care?" He held his breath as he waited for a reply.

She shrugged. "Maybe a little."

"Only a little?" he cajoled.

"I'm still mad at you," she exclaimed hotly.

"Think of me saving your dad and your friends as an apology then."

"My dad still won't like you."

"I can live with that," he muttered. So long as she changed her mind about him. "I need something to fight with. I don't suppose you know of a hidden gun stash?"

"There's a panic room built into the closet in the master bedroom, but I doubt the previous owner's left any weapons."

"I wonder if I can make it to my car and get my guns," he mused aloud.

"Won't shooting them draw too much attention?"

"Got a better idea?" he asked.

"Hear the song playing right now?"

"What's that got to do with anything?"

"That's 'Holly Jolly Christmas,' which reminds me of how the mistletoe on the main floor was hung."

With invisible fishing line, strong enough to act as a garrotte, and it just so happened there was a spool of it in the craft room.

Armed with that, a few knitting needles, and beads—and feeling a bit like that kid in the *Home Alone* movie—he climbed into the laundry chute in the master bedroom bathroom. A tighter fit than he liked, but he'd traveled through worse.

It helped that Blake gave him a long, hot kiss and said, "Be careful," before he went down.

"I intend to." Because if he could be her hero and save them all, maybe they'd be spending Christmas together in bed.

He inched down the laundry chute, hands and feet spread so he didn't slide. Lucky for him, it had an opening on the main floor.

He shoved at the hatch just enough to spy on the situation. The mudroom appeared empty, the doors to it shut. Three in total. Garage, backyard, and swinging panel into the kitchen.

Easing out of the chute, he put his ear to the kitchen door and listened. Heard the faint strains of Christmas music and not much else.

He eased it open enough to give him a peek at the kitchen sink and part of the island. He did not have a line of sight on the great room where people were being held, nor any idea how many elves were involved. He'd not kept count of the staff wandering through the party, but he knew it was more than four. Fuck, now that he replayed the faces he'd seen, more like eight. A gun would have really helped those odds.

Over the Christmas music still incongruously playing, he heard the distinct sound of someone throwing up, which led to some yelling.

"That's fucking disgusting!"

Mathias took a chance and peeked around the corner of the mudroom door and was in time to see Joleen as she lifted her head from the vase she'd puked in. She weaved on her feet and still looked green as she barked back, "Don't you dare be pissed. You're the one that drugged us."

The guy in elven green and red tassels didn't seem swayed by the argument. "Get your ass outside if you're going to ralph. And take your puke bucket with you."

"Fuck you. You carry it." Joleen's head snapped, as she did nothing to avoid the slam of the gun into her jaw.

Having watched many a fight, Mathias could tell she'd expected the blow and exaggerated the result. She hit the floor on her knees, head hanging, moaning, "I think I'm going to puke again."

"Get her outside! Now!" barked the leader, looking incongruous with his curly-toed slippers. Since there were only two exits from the house, Mathias quickly ducked back inside, hugged the edge of the door, and waited.

When he heard the grumbling approaching, he hoped Joleen knew better than to react if she saw him.

Her gaze remained straight ahead, as did her captor's. He never even saw Mathias, but the asshole who thought it was okay to ruin a party felt the string as it went around his neck. Mathias cut off any sound he might have made, pulling hard and twisting.

Joleen whirled, dropping into a fighting stance,

proving she'd not been as sick as she faked. Only when the body hit the floor did she whisper, "Where's Blake?"

"Hiding upstairs."

"Got a spare gun?"

"That's the only one." He pointed to weapon still held in the dead man's hand and asked, "How many targets?"

Joleen snared it. "Four that I know of still inside. But from the way they were talking, we can expect a few outside."

He grimaced. "I've got two more guns in my car, but I'm parked at least twenty yards from the house." Because they'd arrived last.

"Meaning we might be spotted and the trash inside might start shooting."

"Will they?" he asked.

She rubbed her jaw. "It only takes one to start."

Then the mass hysteria snowball effect would hit and there could be a bloodbath. "What do they want?"

"Only fifty million dollars."

His brows shot up to the stratosphere. "Fuck, they aren't aiming for small change." But they'd picked the right party to hold hostage. The guests could probably scrape that amount together. "Do you think they'll walk away if they get it?"

Joleen shrugged. "Maybe."

Maybe wasn't good enough. Not when Blake was counting on him.

"We need to thin them out."

"You have a plan?"

"Yeah, but one of us is gonna get a little chilly."

CHAPTER FOURTEEN

Down through the chimney, dropping a gun, to take out the assholes ruining the fun.

Rather than wait inside the bathroom, Blake chose to head for the panic room to see if its emergency line still worked.

It didn't.

Apparently, the elves had been busy, and one had snuck upstairs to cut the line. They'd obviously planned this for a while and sprung the plan into action the moment Ariel hired the caterers, but were they thieves of opportunity? Or the same kind of killers that had invaded her house once upon a time and murdered a young mother?

She would rather die than lose someone she loved again. For all she knew, everyone was already dead. What if she was the only one left?

Huff. Pant. Huff.

Panic, quickening her heart, dampening her palms. It had been awhile since she'd had to do her breathing exercises. It took years of therapy before she could sleep without nightmares and stopped flinching every time she heard a noise at the door.

Undone because, once more, she was a victim of senseless crime.

Her father was in the midst of it. As were so many of her friends. And her lover had gone to deal with it.

Could she really be a coward who hid rather than acted? But what could she do? She'd not been joking when she said her body wasn't made for fighting. Despite her father's best attempts, she'd failed even the most basic self-defense lessons. Lacked the killer instinct. Tended to hyperventilate and freeze when scared. Just like when she was a little girl.

History was doomed to repeat itself because she never learned how to take someone's life.

She paced the small panic room, the door shut but not sealed. It didn't hold much. A pair of chairs. A table. Cupboards, which, when opened, showed bottled water. Packaged snacks. A useless phone bolted to the wall, and the safe, currently closed. But she knew the combination unless Hugo and Ariel had already changed it.

For some reason she keyed in the numbers, and it clicked as it unlocked. Pulling it open, she stared. Not at the rubber-banded stacks of cash but the gun inside. Just a single revolver, but she pulled it out. Could she use it?

She'd probably punch herself in the face again if she tried. Her father had tried to warn her about recoil, but the first time she fired one at the range, she still screamed and hit herself when it went off.

She never went back. Guns equaled death. She almost put it back in the safe, only to pause. She couldn't use it, but she knew people downstairs who could. The problem being, how to get the gun into their hands?

Pop.

She jumped at the single gunshot, almost dropping the revolver on her foot. Not the time to be clumsy.

Bang.

"Argh." The gunfire and yelling came from outside the panic room, whose door she'd yet to close.

Had Matt gotten his hands on a gun? Was he the one who'd cried out?

The lights in the house went out abruptly. She froze in place, heart pounding. She couldn't let fear control her. She crept out of the panic room to the bedroom door and peeked out. Heard voices.

"No one goes outside. Not until we're done here," someone barked.

She dropped to her knees and crawled to the edge of the wall, where it met the railing that overlooked the great room, and listened out of sight as the same guy demanded, "Transfer the fucking money now or else."

Hugo's voice remained calm, if thick, as he replied, "As you can see, I'm trying. We're having connectivity issues."

She dared a glance. Candles burning in the room allowed her to see the guests crowded in front of the fireplace. Many of them slumped. A few sobbing. The waiters, a handful scattered throughout the room and armed with guns, still wore their ridiculous elf costumes. It added a sense of surrealism to the scene.

"Maybe if my friend over here takes your wife for a walk up to your bedroom for some playtime you'll figure out a way to fix it," threatened one of the attackers.

"Lay a hand on me and you'll lose it," Ariel challenged, the words slurred with bravado and eggnog.

"Shut the fuck up." A different fellow leveled his gun on her. "Let me shoot her. Maybe then they'll stop being so fucking mouthy."

"Why not pick on someone more your size?" blustered her dad.

Pride filled her that he would stand up for what was right. Fear, too, because courage didn't make him impervious to danger.

"Mind your fucking business."

"Or what?" Daddy surged forward, brave as the day he'd saved her. Maybe he could—

Bang.

She put a hand to her mouth and held in a cry as her father crumpled, holding his leg.

No. Not again. Time to stop screwing around. She had a gun but lacked the ability to hit anything from here. She'd never make it down those stairs unnoticed, and while the laundry chute remained an option, she feared either getting wedged in the space—because for all she knew Mathias was stuck in there—or slipping and accidentally shooting herself.

The glow of the fire in the hearth caught her eye. The home invaders had their hostages clustered in front of it, giving her an idea. Probably a really bad one, yet she didn't see any other choice. She had to act. Daddy was bleeding. Matt was missing. More people might get shot.

She bundled the gun and some water bottles into a pillowcase she stripped from the bed and emerged onto the balcony overlooking the steep incline down to the lake. She wasn't going down but up. Seeing the fireplace gave her an idea.

She slipped off her shoes to give herself better traction to stand on the wide black metal railing with its clear glass panel. Praying she wouldn't slip, she reached for the roofline. Lucky for her, it sloped, and the railing gave enough height she could grip the roof and hike her knee high enough to kneel on it. Then the other. She'd looped the pillowcase with her stash on her belt. It dragged behind her as she crawled.

The asphalt shingle roof proved rough and icy. Too cold for just a dress. She could have used her boots or mittens but had no time to waste. She'd be a hell of a lot chillier if she were six feet under.

She quickly scrabbled up the peak of the roof, the tips of her fingers numb from the cold. A good thing because she had a feeling they were being scraped raw. The big chimney smoked, the fire in it burning happily. Meaning she couldn't just dump a gun down that chute. That never went well in the movies. She had to extinguish it first.

She pulled out the water bottles she'd brought along. Uncapping them all, she set them on their side so they could pour down. Immediately the thin smoke thickened, a dark, billowing mass that brought a tickle to her throat and a sting to her eyes.

She couldn't stop now. She uncapped and dropped the last few bottles but for one. The last was quickly poured over the pillowcase. Hoping the gun could handle getting wet, she wrapped the pillowcase around it, and then she sent it down the chimney. Fingers and toes crossed someone would notice and use it. Praying even harder it didn't go off and accidentally shoot someone she liked.

Eyes streaming, she sat on her butt and began scooting to the edge of the roof. *Don't slide. Don't fall.*

When she got to the spot where she'd climbed up, she flipped onto her belly and shimmied until her legs dangled. Pushing a bit more dragged her dress up, meaning her ass was exposed and her cheeks chilly, because those snowman panties were cute, not practical.

But she was almost safe. Just a bit farther.

"Fucking cunt!" was the only warning she got before she was yanked from her perch and slammed into the balcony.

CHAPTER FIFTEEN

Winters, the Iceman, sensed something was wrong that day. So with a smoking gun, he took off at a run, ready to blow a fucker away.

WHEN THE FIREPLACE BEGAN TO SMOKE, IT WAS just another clusterfuck of things that had gone wrong since Mathias went down the laundry chute.

It didn't start out that way. After taking out the guy in the mudroom, Mathias and Joleen had quickly devised a plan. She'd take the gun and provide a distraction outdoors, drawing some of the attackers out of the room, while he did something about the power. Unfortunately, it didn't go as planned.

The leader of the elves—who really should have dressed as Santa if he was calling the shots—didn't fall for it. The Boss kept his gun and indoor henchman—whom Mathias mentally nicknamed Bucky, Snauzer, and Fatass—focused on the guests.

The Boss—who'd obviously been spoiled as a child given the tantrum he was throwing—was losing his shit because Hugo claimed he didn't have internet to do what they wanted. The signal was pretty shit up here. How long before the thugs stopped asking and started hurting?

Pop. Snap. "Argh!"

The noise from outside penetrated the music, and The Boss lifted his head like a hound getting his scent.

"Want me to go check and see if Joe is all right?" Bucky asked.

Joe was not. Joe was currently sleeping with the laundry in the basement.

The Boss shook his head. "He probably just shot that puking bitch. Everyone stays here. And you stop dicking me around. Give me my money."

"I'll do it," one of the guests offered, looking pale and sweaty.

Idiot. If Hugo couldn't connect, neither could he. But it might take a few minutes before The Boss realized it.

Mathias moved back to the mudroom. Slipping into the laundry chute, he took it down one more level to the basement, avoiding Joe's face when he arrived in the bin at the bottom.

Unlike the rest of the house, the basement was bland and unfinished. Stone block walls, cement floor. The furnace hummed as it pushed hot air, trying to keep ahead of the cold outside. His goal was the electrical panel.

Time things got even more confusing. The longer they stalled the home invaders, the better chance they had of the guests snapping out of their semi-drugged state and able to fight.

He flipped the main switch, and everything went out. Lights, the furnace, every single electrical hum in the place went dead, and in that quiet he heard nothing.

Which he found more ominous than anything. He'd expected yelling at the least, a bit of panicked shooting at the worst.

Nothing.

It took him a moment to adjust his eyesight, and even then, he walked arms out until he reached the stairs. As he was climbing, he heard a gunshot.

Fuck.

He moved quickly, listening for only a second before slipping into the mudroom. As he put his ear to the swinging door to the kitchen, it suddenly opened and clocked him.

He reeled, ears ringing.

Then someone was swinging at him and yelling, "There's someone in the kitchen!"

He'd lost the element of surprise. He hooked his fist and thrust upward, catching the guy in the gut. He kept pummeling the fellow until he slumped to the floor. Matt recognized him. It was the one he'd called Snauzer.

Click. A muzzle prodded the back of his head, and he raised his hands.

"Yeah, you better keep those where I can see them. Let's go, asshole." Bucky prodded him in the direction of the kitchen and the other guests. Given the muzzle on his head never wavered, Mathias chose to bide his time in the interest of avoiding spillage of his brains on the wide-plank oak floors.

The many lit candles gave light and shadow to the room. The Boss half turned to face him.

"Where did you come from?"

"That's the dude who had the fight with his girlfriend," Fatass remarked. "The curvy chick in the snowman dress."

"Where is your ho?" Bucky asked.

"We had a fight. She left. Guess I won't be getting shit for Christmas," Mathias lied.

The Boss didn't buy it. "Bullshit. All the cars are still here."

"Should I go looking for her?" Bucky appeared a little too eager.

"Don't you fucking touch her!" Roarke yelled, as he surged to his feet. His leg was bleeding, soaking his flashy sequined pants. Not the worse wound. He'd live if he got medical attention, but he didn't imagine Blake would be too happy about it.

No need to guess who shot him, given Bucky yelled, "You want another? Keep running your mouth and I'll fucking shoot you in the head this time, old man."

A haggard-looking Roarke growled but sat back down, and Mathias joined him on the hearth. As The Boss argued with his crew, Mathias managed a quiet, "She's hiding upstairs."

"You should have stayed with her. I had this," the older guy said.

Mathias eyed the bleeding leg. "I can see that. What did I miss?"

"The incompetent idiots thought they could wave some guns around and intimidate everyone into giving them money."

"It appears to not be working."

Roarke smirked. "They might have drugged us, but we're not fucking amateurs. Ariel activated a signal disruptor before they took her phone."

"Why not take them out?"

"Because I'm seeing double for one. The fuckers drugged the punch."

"Not everyone was drinking."

"Too many sober civilians."

They could scrub a lot from the public records, but eyewitness accounts? More problematic.

"Nobody knows me," he remarked quietly.

"No, but you're useless sitting here with me. So much for your marksman skills."

"I let Joleen have the gun," he grumbled.

"You only brought one gun?" Roarke asked.

"It's more than you bothered to bring."

"It didn't go with the outfit," admitted the older man. "Might have been hard to explain to my girlfriend. She's got a thing for the king and has been groping me all night."

The problem with dating non-mercenaries was they tended to freak out and ask things like, "Why do you own a gun? Have you ever killed someone? Why is your home booby-trapped?"

"Is anyone armed?"

"I've got a small knife strapped to my ankle, and I'm sure a few others have stuff on them, but we have to be cautious. Civilians are watching," Roarke reminded. Some of the wealthy guests might be taken aback to see people they knew taking out criminals.

"They're getting pissy," Mathias observed as The Boss screamed, "Transfer the fucking money *now*!"

"I can't," blubbered the man who'd offered to pay. "It's not working."

"You're fucking lying." The gun lifted and aimed for the fellow's head.

Hugo stepped in. "It's not his fault. Our phones aren't connecting."

It was Fatass—who probably spent a lot of time gaming online when not holding people hostage—who said, "Fancy place like this has gotta have internet. Get him to use his home computer."

Hugo shrugged. "Actually, I don't have anything set up yet. Just moved in and all."

"Jesus fucking Christ. You're a fucking billionaire. I thought you assholes were connected to the net twenty-four fucking seven," The Boss ranted.

"Maybe someone could give him a hotspot?" a sniffling blonde suggested.

She and a few others looked genuinely terrified. He could almost make a game of guessing who was a merc versus a civvie.

"Don't be stupid. No one has any service," said a brunette, who looked more excited than properly scared.

"There's such a thing as a satellite phone, you know," argued the blonde with mascara streaks funneling down her cheeks.

"Would you shut the fuck up?" The Boss was losing his patience, and Bucky grinned as he swung the muzzle of his gun back and forth, itching for a reason to use it.

Pshhhhh. There was a loud sizzle, and then billowing smoke steamed out from behind the fire screen as more water landed on the live fire.

"What the fuck now?" screamed The Boss before hacking.

Mathias shut his stinging eyes against the smoke. Heard the yelling, the coughing.

In the commotion that followed, Matt lunged toward the last place he'd recalled seeing Snauzer and a gun fired. Since he didn't feel any pain, it didn't appear to be aimed at him.

"Hugo!" Ariel screamed, identifying the victim.

It subdued the still drugged crowd, just like the gun pointed at his face had Matt lacing fingers over his head again and marching to join the rest of them. He sat on the sooty hearth as The Boss screamed that someone had to be on the roof. Bucky went upstairs to check, and Matt went cold. Surely Blake had hidden herself?

A hacking cough drew his attention to the dirty hearth. Someone had poured water down the chimney. He wanted to say Joleen did it as part of her diversion, but what if she hadn't?

What if... He glanced at the stairs then back at the fireplace, noticing the odd lump lying in it. Roarke sat nearby, putting pressure on his leg.

"Cover me," Matt whispered, having a sudden curiosity.

Roarke didn't question; he just began making a scene, bellowing about how he couldn't feel his leg. And he needed help. And whiskey. Maybe a joint.

It drew attention to the wounded man as Mathias leaned to grab the sodden lump in the hearth. The fabric tore the moment he tugged, but it held long enough to reveal the present inside the sack.

"Someone shut him the fuck up!" The Boss bellowed.

“Maybe we should shoot him?” A dubious suggestion by Snauzer.

“Go ahead.”

“You go ahead. You said this would be a simple robbery.”

“Did you think the guns were just for show?” was The Boss’ sarcastic reply.

As they argued, Mathias tucked the gun into the back of his pants. Then he lunged forward and slapped Roarke, exclaiming, “Get a grip!”

That quieted the older man, who glared.

“About fucking time,” The Boss said. “Couldn’t hear myself think.”

“Because you were acting so intelligent before,” someone muttered.

“Who said that?” The Boss glared at everyone suspiciously before snorting in disgust. “I’ve fucking had it. No more dicking around. Since the signal is shit in the mountains, let’s take a few of them to town. Grab Laurentian’s wife and those two.” He pointed to some guests.

Mathias could have sworn he heard a scream from upstairs. He’d run out of time. “Hey, asshole, I think we’re all tired of listening to your useless lips flapping.” As he stepped past Ariel, he nudged her and dropped a knitting needle into her lap.

“Sit down—” The Boss opened his yap, and Mathias shut it.

Bang!

He immediately ducked and whirled, aiming for Snauzer next, but the man moved, and his shot missed. His second one didn't, and another attacker went down. As for Fatass? He blubbered on the floor. Ariel stood over him with the knitting needle, the end of it bloody.

The blonde was in absolute hysterics. The brunette gaped, mouth and eyes wide open. While Roarke bellowed, "Blake!"

As if Mathias needed a reminder there was still at least one invader in the house.

He bolted for the stairs and took them two at a time as he pounded to the second floor then down the hall to the master bedroom. He halted upon seeing Blake through the window, outside on the balcony, held in a chokehold by the same asshole who'd taken Mathias prisoner.

Bucky was about to regret the choices he'd made in life.

"Drop it!" Bucky screamed. "Or I will blow her brains out."

Mathias set the gun down in plain sight before he entered the room, hands raised. "Let her go. You've lost."

"Not while I have a hostage, I haven't. Rich mother fuckers. I thought Barry was nuts when he suggested coming after a bunch of you bastards, but look at this place. This bedroom is probably worth more than I make in a year."

"Not a reason to steal it."

"It's redistributing. It's not fair you fuckers get all the nice shit and the breaks."

"Breaks?" He snorted, taking a single step. "I was in the foster care system. I worked my ass off for the things I have. And so did those people downstairs."

Blake's eyes were shiny with fear, but she kept her gaze on him. His Blake, who—given the snow clinging to her and the rawness of her skin—was the stupid, brave soul up on the rooftop.

"I'm tired of working. My bosses always end up being assholes."

"Says the guy holding a woman hostage. Big man, eh?" Mathias taunted.

"I should have shot you earlier." Bucky shoved Blake to the side, and she stumbled, hitting the ground with her knees as the gun in asshole's other hand aimed at Mathias.

This would hurt if he didn't move fast. A slight twitch gave him all the warning he needed to duck the bullet that sailed overhead.

Blake screamed, "No!" and then lunged, shoving the guy hard enough he toppled over the balcony railing, his scream cut short when he landed.

A half-second later, Mathias had her in his arms. "Fuck me, are you okay?" he asked before grabbing her by the cheeks to give her a hot kiss.

She trembled in his arms. "Yes. No. I'm going to have some scrapes and bruises."

"You were the one who dropped that stuff down the chimney," he stated.

She nodded.

He glanced up and inwardly shuddered. That would have been a nasty fall if she'd slipped. "You saved us," he told her, knowing she needed something to bolster her. He could see how fragile she was now. Close to coming apart.

"My dad?"

"Is injured but I suspect he'll recover. Hugo, though, might be a tad more serious."

"And the bad guys?"

He shook his head.

"They're all dead," she whispered, her gaze going to the railing. He brought it back to focus on him.

"Don't you dare feel bad about what you had to do."

She pressed her face to his chest. "I couldn't let him shoot you. Couldn't."

She shook in his arms as he carried her back inside the bedroom, only to see Roarke leaning in the doorway, a gun loosely held in his hand, a belt strapped tight above the wound on his leg.

"Blake." The man sounded broken.

With a cry, Blake swung out of Mathias's arms and ran to her father. "Daddy! Are you okay?"

"'Tis but a flesh wound." Roarke kept his tone light.

Blake burst into tears.

Father and daughter hugged, but over her head, Roarke said, "You need to get out of here."

"Still trying to get rid of me?" Mathias said with a sneer. "Why don't we ask Blake what she wants?"

"I want him to stay, Daddy," she sniffled.

"I wouldn't recommend it. The cops are on their way."

No need to say more.

Her shoulders slumped. "Oh."

Mathias could see the torn expression on Roarke's face. Then the resignation. "I'm gonna see if that bathroom has any gauze for my leg." A not so subtle attempt to leave them alone.

Roarke limped off, and Blake hugged herself. "I guess this is goodbye."

"I don't want to leave," he said as he crossed the room in long strides and pulled her into his arms.

She sighed against him. "And I wish you didn't have to go."

"Not much of a choice. I killed at least three men downstairs, and if anyone asks, I tossed the guy off the balcony, too."

"I am not going to let you take the blame. I did it. I'll tell the police it was self-defense."

"Don't do that. What if you get a dick DA?"

"I have to. You don't understand. I'm a terrible liar."

Was she seriously going to argue? He imagined he could hear the sirens. He had to leave now while he could. But what of Blake? There was so much left to say.

Only one thing left for him to do.

Winters the Iceman had to hurry on his way, before the cops could come, and ruin his fun, he kidnapped Blake and ran away.

CHAPTER SIXTEEN

Come on, it's lovely weather for a car ride and kidnapping by you.

Blake could have protested when Matt tossed her over her shoulder. At the very least she could have yelled for her father. Instead, as Matt jogged down the steps, she tried to quell her shaking.

She'd killed a man.

To save another.

No one she cared about had died today. And Mathias was abducting her she realized as he hit the main floor.

It was Joleen who said, "Hey, what are you doing with Blake?"

"Making sure she doesn't have to lie. I hear she sucks at it."

"Good plan," was Joleen's helpful reply.

As for the rest, they seemed more interested in

discussing the brazenness of today's thieves as Matt strutted out the door.

"Where are we going?" she asked as he tossed her into his car.

"Somewhere that isn't here." The tires spun as he sped away.

"Are you making me a felon fleeing the cops?" she asked as he turned off onto a side road before the distant flashing lights could pass them.

"I'm taking you somewhere safe."

"My dad needs me."

"I need you, too."

"Why? Do you still have a use for me?" She hadn't quite forgotten the revelations of earlier. What he'd done to save them didn't fix everything.

He slammed on the brakes, jolting them both, and for a moment, as he gripped the wheel so hard, she wondered if he'd bend it.

Slowly, he took a breath and said, "Honestly? I didn't need you to accomplish my mission."

"How else would you have met Hugo?"

He snorted. "Would you like me to count the ways? I could have found out when his private jet was arriving and met him at the airport. Knocked on his door and handed it over. Broken into his house and left it on his pillow."

"So why seduce me?"

"Because I couldn't help myself." The man looking at her with emotion was anything but cold.

That name, Iceman, didn't describe the person she'd come to know.

"And now that your mission is done?"

"I still want you."

"What makes you think I feel the same?"

"Tell me you don't and I'll leave you alone. Right now."

She glanced around. "In the middle of nowhere?"

"You know what I mean. If you don't want to see me again, then I'll leave for good and never bother you again."

"What if I don't want that?" She picked at a loose thread on her ruined dress. "I like you, Matt. A lot."

"I'm a killer, Blake."

"So's my dad." She shrugged. "If I can love him, then..." She caught herself and blushed hard before stammering, "I'm not saying I love you. It's too soon. I—"

He leaned over the console to kiss her. "Shut up."

"But..."

"Seriously, Blake. We don't need to say anything more right now other than let's give this thing a chance."

"So I shouldn't say that I'm feeling very warm and fuzzy toward you right now? And horny. How fast can you make it to town?"

"Not as fast as I'd like, given where your hand is sitting," he growled, putting the car into gear.

"You might want to stay parked for a few more minutes," she purred as she unzipped his pants.

"Here?"

"Got a problem with steaming the windows in your rental?"

"No."

His voice didn't sound steady as she grabbed his cock in her hands and squeezed him tight. The hard flesh throbbed in her grip, the tip pearling. She undid her seatbelt and leaned over, lapping at the salty drop, hearing him suck in a breath.

When she peeked at him, it was to see him staring at her, groaning as she bathed the head of his dick with her tongue. Then, with one hand pumping him, she took him into her mouth and sucked.

He groaned. "Fuck, yes."

She worked his cock, pumping it, sucking it, making it hard and ready. She explored every intimate inch of it, using her tongue to trace the pulsing veins, her lips to tease the soft skin of the head. Only when he panted and appeared as if he'd explode did she finally hike up her dress and straddle him.

"Yes," he hissed.

She bounced on his dick, feeling the steering wheel at her back, his hands on her waist, her head pressing against the roof of the car. It wasn't easy to move, but he helped, thrusting up into her, finding her sweet spot. Hitting it over and over again.

As she gasped, he completely took over, his grip on her rocking her on his shaft, driving himself deep. She gasped in pleasure as her clit rubbed against him. Her pussy quivered. Clenching. Her orgasm built inside.

Faster, he slid her back and forth, increasing the friction. Bringing her to the edge.

She opened her heavily lidded eyes just before climax and found him staring at her.

Their gazes remained locked as she hurtled for the edge of pleasure. He rocked into her faster, and her orgasm hit. She screamed. He yelled.

She collapsed in his arms, breathing hard.

Then erupted into giggles when someone rapped on the window. She scrambled into her seat, yanking down her dress while he did his best to cover his sticky cock.

The cop wasn't dumb. He knew what they'd been doing and gave them a friendly warning about parking on the side of the road without hazard lights then wished them a Merry Christmas.

Little did he know Blake already had the only present she needed in the man beside her.

EPILOGUE

Thumpity. Thump, thump, thumpity, thump. Winters fell in love. Thumpity. Thump, thump, thumpity, thump. It's that or he's really drunk. Winters, the Iceman, had his heart melt hard that day, and now everyone knows he will drop you dead if you try to take his Blake away.

ON CHRISTMAS MORNING, BLAKE WOKE TO FIND a tree in her living room. Not just any tree, a purple tree with multi-colored lights, a flashing star, and a present beneath it.

"Where did that come from?" she asked, eyeing it with her head canted to the side. "Did you steal someone's Christmas tree?"

"It would have been a nicer looking one if I had." Rather than being a Scrooge, he'd overpaid for the monstrosity.

"Why?" Her tone was incredulous.

It seemed obvious. "Because you didn't have one."

"For a good reason. Fluff will destroy it."

Indeed, the cat eyed it with evil intent. He couldn't wait to watch. "Doesn't she deserve some fun, too? Besides, you needed a tree so I could have a place for your present."

"You didn't have to get me anything."

"You're right, I didn't have to. I wanted to." Which was a whole different ball game. Turned out he didn't hate Christmas as much as he hated having no one to celebrate it with. "You going to open it?"

"Given the size of that gift, it better not be a ring. We've not been dating long enough," she exclaimed, and yet he saw the tremble in her clasped hands.

He didn't admit he'd glanced at a few. He eased her worry instead. "It's not a ring."

"Then what is it?"

"Open the box and find out."

"In a second. Hold on. I got you something, too." She left, only to return a few minutes later with a box tied with a bright red ribbon.

"You first," he insisted, even as curiosity was killing him. He didn't remember the last time someone gave him a gift for Christmas. As a kid in foster care, the best he got was a few used toys and clothes at Christmas.

She pried open the tiny box. Stared for a second then chuckled before pulling out the necklace with its holiday-themed pendant.

"I love it!" she said with a wide smile.

Only she could. He remembered seeing it and wondering who would buy such an ugly piece of jewelry. It was Joleen who'd told him that Blake had admired it, so he'd overpaid for the metal snowman, hand-crafted and inset with tiny stones dangling off a chain of gold.

"Help me put it on." She turned around that he might latch it around her neck, always trusting him. He dragged his fingers over her nape. His lips followed, and he felt her shiver.

"Not yet," she said, turning with a grin. "Time for your present."

She pushed it into his lap. It didn't weigh much but was much larger than the gift he'd given her. He tugged the ribbon and then paused to smile as Fluff attacked it. Only when the cat yanked it from his hand and ran off with it did he finally open the box. He stared inside before saying, "What the fuck am I looking at?" He held up a large black button then a carrot.

Looking mischievous, Blake winked and said, "Do you want to build a snowman?"

He did. His very first one. The best the world had ever seen, according to Blake.

He made love to Blake right after and spent the night. Two days later, they finally decided to empty his hotel room since he wasn't using it.

On New Year's Eve, he pulled out another small

box just before midnight. Before his knee even hit the floor, she said yes.

And his heart swelled to ten times its size.

I HOPE you enjoyed this little Bad Boy Holiday treat. Nothing like getting a killer to fall in love. Merry Christmas and Happy New Year. ~Eve

READY FOR A BAD BOY SPIN-OFF? CHECK OUT KILLER MOMS STARTING WITH *SOCCER MOM*.

More books at EveLanglais.com

Made in the USA
Columbia, SC
06 October 2021

46791697R00090